# Magic and Mischief

Emily Martha Sorensen

Magic and Mischief
Copyright © 2018 by Emily Martha Sorensen
Cover and internal art by Emily Martha Sorensen

All rights reserved.  Printed in the United States of America.

ISBN-13: 978-1-949607-00-0
ISBN-10: 1-949607-00-3

http://www.emilymarthasorensen.com

Also by Emily Martha Sorensen

Standalones:
*Black Magic Academy*

Fairy Senses:
*Fairy Eyeglasses*
*Fairy Compass*
*Fairy Earmuffs*
*Fairy Barometer*
*Fairy Pox*
*Fairy Slippers*
*Fairy Lunchbox*
*Fairy Icepack*
*Fairy Stopwatch*
*Fairy Toothbrush*
*Fairy Perfume*

Dragon Eggs:
*Dragon's Egg*
*Dragon's Hope*
*Dragon's First Christmas*
*Dragon's Fire*

Comics:
*A Magical Roommate*
*To Prevent World Peace*

Picture Books:
*Tabby, Tabby, Burning Bright*

The End in the Beginning:
*The Keeper and the Rulership*
*The Fires of the Rulership*
*The Magic or the Rulership*

Trilogy of a Teenage Werevulture:
*Trials of a Teenage Werevulture*
*Trifles of a Teenage Werevulture*

The Numbers Just Keep
Getting Bigger:
*Twenty-Four Potential*
*Children of Prophecy*

Not Quite a Harem:
*Not Quite a Curse*

Magical Mayhem:
*To Prevent World Peace*
*To Prevent Chic Costumes*
*To Prevent Clear Paths*
*To Prevent Smart Choices*
*To Prevent Warm Welcomes*
*To Prevent Cute Mascots*

Short Story Collections:
*Worlds of Wonder*

To my brother, Michael,
who totally would have been like
Donovan and Junior
in the Wilkinsons short stories
if he'd thought he could get away with it.

And to my twin sons,
Simon and Nicodemus,
who I hope will never be as mischievous
as those two.

# Table of Contents

# Valentine's Oops

"Oh, by the way, my sister's planning to use a love potion on you."

I looked up from filling our last water balloon in the bathroom sink. "What?"

Junior made a smoochy face. "Elsie and Donovan, sittin' in a tree. K-I-S-S-I-N-G —"

I threw my water balloon at his smug face. This resulted in an all-out battle to the drenched, finishing with both of us left dripping and my sister's teddy bear still on the chair we'd set it up on, bone-dry.

This seemed unfair, so I tipped it off the chair and into the soaked rug. *Hmm, I wonder if Mom's gonna object that we had a water balloon fight in the hallway.*

"Anyway, like I was saying." Junior cleared his throat. "Elsie and Donovan, sittin' in a tree! K-I—"

I grabbed the teddy bear and threw it at his head.

Junior caught it. "Does that mean you don't want her attention?" he asked, grinning. His eyes were glowing yellow with mischief. All the Wilkinsons' eyes changed color sometimes. Just like weird things happened around them all the time.

"Of course I don't!" I cried. "Elsie's just like Genevieve! How'd you like it if my sister tried to chase you?"

Junior shuddered. His eyes turned back to the same brown as his skin.

"Well, maybe love potions don't exist," I said hopefully. "I've never seen one, have you?"

"I'd never seen Alyssa turn into a walrus before last week, either," Junior said.

I grinned. That had been *awesome.* Huge tusks on Junior's baby sister for a whole hour. I don't know why their mom had been so upset. She was the one who left that Beatles song playing.

"Okay, well, maybe it wasn't a love potion," I said. "What was she doing?"

"She was sorting the candy hearts that said 'BE MINE' into a bowl. And she was chanting the titles of romance movies. And she drew Xs and Os all over a Valentine's card with your name on it."

I put my head in my hands. I was doomed.

My doom was delivered to me in a card that had Disney princesses on it. I didn't know which was worse, the doom or the princesses.

*I am so not gonna eat those,* I thought, stripping a box of candy hearts off the back.

"Hey, Joe," I asked the kid behind me, rattling the box. "Wanna trade?"

His eyes lit up, and the sucker swapped me a heart-shaped lollipop. Sweet.

I chomped on it while he crunched the hearts, and I watched him surreptitiously. He didn't break into song or run to Elsie's classroom to declare his undying love for her, so perhaps I'd have to wait till recess to see the effects.

I waited impatiently through math and spelling, dying to meet Junior on the playground and ask if he knew anything else about his sister's plans for the day. She was sure to try something else. The Wilkinsons didn't give up easily.

By the time the recess bell rang, I was going crazy.

*Maybe I should crack an egg on her head,* I thought, drumming my fingers on the desk. *Maybe I should put chewing gum in her desk. Maybe I should behead her Barbies — oh, wait, Junior and I did that already.*

How was I supposed to drive her away when I'd already done everything?

I shoved my way through the crowded hallway and pushed past other kids to get to the door. Junior's class must have let out a minute earlier, because he was already waiting outside for me. His eyes were orange with intensity.

"I don't think she's got me yet," I hissed, scanning the playground for his sister.

"She still might," Junior whispered. "I saw her smuggle a doll in her backpack today."

*A doll?* I spied Elsie standing in a group of six girls, one of them my sister. Her shirt looked suspiciously bulgy, like she'd hidden something under there. *What's the big deal about . . .*

One of the supervising teachers turned her back on our side of the playground to break up a fight over a kicked soccer ball. Another turned her back to check up on a wuss who was crying about the soccer ball hitting him.

The instant they were looking away, Elsie whipped the doll out of her shirt and tossed it up in the air. It hovered and then flapped a pair of construction-paper wings. From a distance, I could see she'd put one of her baby sister's diapers on it.

*Oh, NO WAY,* I thought.

The thing zoomed up in the air, reached into a purse she'd strapped on its back, and pulled out a handful of candy hearts.

"RUN!" Junior and I screamed, and we scattered.

The doll dove straight down for us, and hail of colored candy pelted at us. I barely dodged as a white *WHY NOT* whammed the dirt by my feet. A yellow *HUG ME* thwacked into the swingset, and three pink hearts I couldn't read dinged across the jungle gym as I ran past.

*Save me!* I thought, panicking. *Save me, save me, save me!*

Several other kids had noticed the doll and were shouting and running. One fatso boy from Elsie's class was outpacing me.

"What's this?" one of the teachers demanded, marching over. The doll dropped like a stone. "Who threw this?" she demanded, seizing it and holding it up.

Silence. Dead silence. Everyone knew you didn't tell the teachers such things: there was a *code.*

"Elsie did it!" I said immediately, shooting my hand in the air.

As the teacher turned to start berating Elsie, I relaxed. If there was any certain way to make her hate me, that would be it.

"Thanks a lot, you jerk," Elsie growled, glaring at me as we waited for the school bus to go back home. "Thanks to you, I have to go to detention tomorrow. The only reason I didn't have to today is because I have Brownies!"

I shrugged. Junior almost always had detention, and I did half the time. Big whoop.

"You shouldn't have sent that cupid after me," I shot back.

"*You?* You think I like *you?*" Elsie shrieked. "You stupid moron! You're just like my brother! And you ruined my cupcakes last week!"

We'd made the bowl dump cupcake goo all over her head when the baseball game on TV had said "Batter up!" I'd forgotten all about that. It had been funny.

"Junior saw you chanting love spells over a Valentine's card with my name on it," I accused. "Explain that."

"Stupid!" Elsie hissed, clenching her fists. Her eyes had gone light pink with embarrassment. "That wasn't you. That was Donovan in my *class!*"

"There's a Donovan in your class?" I asked, dumbfounded. "Who's he?"

Elsie folded her arms and glowered. But her eyes flickered off to the side to a line of kids waiting for another bus. There was only one from her class whose name I didn't know.

"Wait, the *fat* kid? You like *him?*"

"Shush up!" Elsie hissed, waving her hands wildly. "It's none of your business!"

*Uh huh. Wow.* I grinned broadly. *Boy, have we got ammunition on her now.*

Still, I dropped a purple Valentine's heart that said DREAM ON down the back of her T-shirt as soon as she spun away. Just in case.

# To Catch a Leprechaun

We were in the middle of detention when Junior had his greatest idea yet.

"Let's catch a leprechaun!" he cried, spinning around in his chair.

My head shot up from writing *I will not misbehave in class*, which was a total lie, and my pencil spun from my fingers as it rolled to the floor. "Is that actually possible?  Do leprechauns exist?"

"Shhhh!" the teacher at the front of the room said, glaring at us.

"Dunno," Junior said, his eyes yellow with mischief, "but wouldn't it be great if they do?  Don't you think we should find out?"

"Totally," I agreed.  "Where do they hang out?"

"At the end of rainbows," Junior said promptly.

"Second warning," the teacher said coldly from the front.

"But where do you find the end of a rainbow?" I asked.  We'd just learned in class that rainbows were giant circles, not arches.  "I mean, circles don't have an end."

"Maybe leprechauns live in the middle," Junior said.

"Hey, yeah!  That would explain why no one ever sees them! 'Cause they're all looking for the end!"

"That's it!" the teacher snapped.  "Another twenty-five lines for each of you.  If you talk again, I'll make it fifty."

I shrugged and picked up my pencil.  We already had three hundred from the little tiny school-sprinklers-spraying-red-fruit-punch-today incident.  It wasn't like another fifty would make that much difference.

As I started writing again, Junior spun around in his seat to give me a thumbs-up.  His eyes were back to the same dark brown as the rest of his face, but they were still glinting with mischief.

*Wish my eyes changed color sometimes,* I thought.  The Wilkinsons were so lucky for being able to do weird things.

My sister and two other girls were over at the Wilkinsons' house by the time we crunched through the snow to get back.

"Hello, Junior," Mrs. Wilkinson called from the kitchen.  "I hear you got detention again."

"Yep," Junior called, throwing his coat at the coat rack.  It missed, so he whistled something tunelessly until it jumped up and hung itself.

Mrs. Wilkinson appeared with her hands on her hips.  The effect was rather ruined by the fact that she had flour on them.  "Boys who go in detention don't get kumquat cookies."

"Awwww," we both complained.

"But I finished half an hour sooner than I usually do!" Junior protested.  "Even though I had more lines than normal!"

"That," she said, "is not a thing to be proud about."

"What about his penmanship grades?" I perked up.  I wanted Junior to get cookies, because if he didn't, I certainly wouldn't.  "He got an A in cursive last week."

"No cookies," Mrs. Wilkinson said.  "And if you don't shape up tomorrow, no cherry tarts either."

"The apple tree is growing cherries again?" I asked excitedly.

She turned her back on me pointedly and headed back to the kitchen.

We passed Junior's sister in the hallway, where she and three friends had set up a Barbie tea party.  Something like a hundred Barbies were all moving in unison, pretending to eat and drink off tiny cups and plates just like the girls were.  It was eerie.

"Hi, Elsie," Junior said.  "Where d'ya keep your suncatcher?"

"Drop dead," Elsie said, not looking up from nibbling from her kumquat cookie.

"What do you need it for?" my sister asked, batting her eyelashes.  Genevieve had recently decided she had a crush on Junior.  It was creepy.

"Leprechaun-catching," Junior said.

"Ooh!" cried Elsie's other two friends.

"Can we play, too?" one of the girls asked excitedly.

"No," Junior said crushingly.  "It's just Donovan and me."

The girls looked disappointed, and Elsie's eyes turned red with irritation. "Fine, you can use my suncatcher, but if you touch anything else in my room, I'll booby-trap your toothbrush," she threatened.

"Not much of a threat if I can see it coming," Junior shrugged.

"Fine, then I'll booby-trap *Dad's* toothbrush and tell him you did it."

I shuddered. That *was* a threat. Junior's dad had gotten all bent out of shape when we'd mixed peanut butter with his shaving cream.

Junior didn't look particularly cowed by this. "Whatever," he said.

We ran up the stairs, and Junior tugged the crystal suncatcher off the window. The suction cup came off with a *pop!*

"Are leprechauns good luck or bad luck?" I asked.

"Don't know," Junior said. "Both, probably."

"Then let's take my sister's four-leaf clover T-shirt," I said. "Maybe it'll help us get the good luck variety."

"Good idea," Junior said.

We got the plastic cauldron Mr. Wilkinson had used for Halloween out of the garage. He'd made it give trick-or-treaters a Fun Size candy bar of any variety the kid requested. We'd gotten it to give us hundreds before Junior's dad had caught on and taken our plastic pumpkins away from us.

"Let's see if it still works," Junior said. He put his face in the bowl and shouted "Gold coins!"

A plastic mesh bag of half a dozen appeared.

"Not bad," Junior grinned, holding it up triumphantly. "Now you try."

"Gold coins," I told the cauldron. Another plastic mesh bag appeared for me. "What're we doing?"

"Baiting the trap," Junior explained. "Leprechauns always have pots of gold at the end of a rainbow, right? Let's trick one into thinking it can steal ours from us."

"Sweet," I said, grinning.

Junior made a teeny circular rainbow with the suncatcher, then he made it bigger by throwing Lucky Charms in the air and shouting

"Four-leaf clover!" over and over again.

We lugged the plastic cauldron into the middle, heavy because of all the chocolate gold coins we'd ripped out of the mesh bags and poured in.

"What do we catch it with?" I grunted, setting it down in the middle with a *paff.* The snow wasn't making it easy, though the ring of rainbow looked pretty cool on top of the white bootprint-churned snow.

Junior pulled out the plastic mesh bags that had held the chocolate coins, and threw them into the air. They turned into one gigantic plastic net.

"Awesome," I said.

"The walnut tree has almonds this week," Junior said. "Wanna climb up there and eat them while we wait?"

"Sure," I said.

So we climbed up the nut tree and munched on almonds. It was easy around Junior, because he didn't have to smash them with a rock to open the shells.

Five minutes later, we were both bored.

"Can't we summon one?" I asked, swinging my legs so that the thick branch under us quivered restlessly. "I don't wanna sit around waiting."

"That seems hard," Junior said. Another minute passed. "Okay, that's long enough," Junior agreed. "Let's try it."

He stood up on the tree limb, crossed his fingers and hopped up and down on it with one leg, pointed down at the cauldron, and shouted, "Leprechaun!"

Something green and little appeared in the cauldron. The mesh net leapt up from the rose bushes and snared it. We gasped and scrambled down from the tree branch, Junior nearly losing his balance and landing on his bottom in the snow.

We crept towards the cauldron, hearts hammering, Junior's eyes pale green with nervousness. We grabbed each end of the plastic net.

"One . . ." he said.

"Two . . ." I said.

"Three!" we shouted, lifting it up.

Inside, we found a leprechaun, complete with green suit, red beard, four-leaf clover in hat, and a tiny black pipe. Unfortunately, it was plastic, from the Tannenbaum house right next door to mine. They always had holiday decorations in the yard, and this looked like one of them.

Junior growled as he pulled it out. We heard giggles behind us, and whirled around.

The girls were standing in the doorway, watching us. Elsie's eyes were hazel with smugness.

"Shush up!" I shouted. "Like you could do better!"

"Try making it a *living* leprechaun," Elsie said, grinning. "Maybe then you'll actually get one."

Junior gritted his teeth as we pulled the net back over the top. This time, we didn't spend time waiting. We just stepped outside the rainbow, he crossed his fingers and hopped up and down on the other leg, and he shouted, "Leprechaun that's a real, living creature!"

The net began to wriggle. Junior and I raced forward to yank it off, and a small dog leapt out and barked at us.

"What the . . .?" Junior asked. "How'd we get *that*?"

I glanced down at the dog's collar and tags. "'Leprechaun,'" I read gloomily.

Junior muttered under his breath and dumped the dog back into the cauldron. "Go back," he said. It vanished.

"Maybe leprechauns don't really exist," one of the girls said. "I've never seen one."

"I haven't either, so they probably don't," Elsie said authoritatively.

"Maybe they're just too stupid to figure out how to summon one," my sister giggled.

That made me mad. "All right, let's go with something little, human-shaped, alive, and magical," I said. "That ought to get *something* interesting!"

Junior nodded and crossed his fingers. He jumped up and down and shouted my suggestion.

We heard a rustle in the cauldron, and the net bobbed up and down.

"A leprechaun?" I asked breathlessly.

"Only one way to find out," Junior said. We inched forward nervously, because of course if this was something magical, we didn't want it flinging anything dangerous at us. We grabbed the edges of the net and threw it off onto the side.

Junior's baby sister poked her head out of top of the cauldron. "Agoogah!" she shouted, holding up a chocolate coin before shoving it in her mouth and trying to chomp on it.

"Magic on the baby means you're all in trouble!" Mrs. Wilkinson thundered from inside.

We scattered.  The girls ran back indoors to their tea party, and I hastily climbed up the nut tree.  Junior was left trying to wrestle the chocolate coins away from the viselike grip of his almost-toddler sister.  She already had chocolate smeared all over her clothes and face.

"I just wanted to capture a leprechaun," Junior protested as his mother stormed up, her eyes red with fury.  "I don't even know if they exist."

"Neither do I, but that's no reason to use magic on your sister," Mrs. Wilkinson snapped, scooping up the baby from the cauldron.

"Agwahhh?" Alyssa said.

A little man appeared in the middle of the cauldron, glanced around with a surprised look, and then vanished.

"Leprechaun?" we both gasped.

"Frankly, I don't care what it was," Mrs. Wilkinson said. "You're both in trouble.  Donovan, get down out of that tree.  I'm calling your mother."

I got down, but my mind was spinning.  I didn't care.  Because I was pretty sure that had been a leprechaun.

After all, it had taken all of the chocolate coins when it disappeared.

# The Goose That Laid Golden Easter Eggs

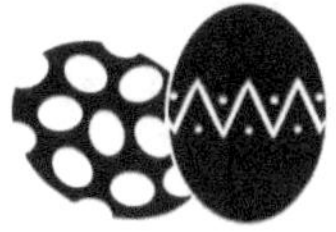

I was really mad at my sister.

"You invited the Wilkinsons over for Easter!  We were supposed to go *there* for Easter!"

"We're always going over there," Genevieve sniffed.  "It's high time we let them come over.  What difference does it make?"

My mouth fell open.  *What difference does it make?*

The Wilkinsons' rose bushes were sprouting jelly beans.  They'd decorated the house with gigantic Peeps and Cadbury creme eggs.  Their lawn had started growing that fake plastic grass you saw in Easter baskets, which was weird even by their standards.  I'd been really looking forward to it!

"Mr. Wilkinson said he would bring the eggs," Genevieve said.

*Oh.*  I calmed down.  Well, that was something.

"And maybe Junior and I can hunt for eggs together," Genevieve giggled.

I glowered at her.  That stupid crush she had on my friend was starting to get annoying.

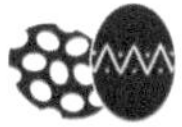

"Thank you for having us over!" Mr. Wilkinson said brightly to my mother.  His hands were behind his back, and something rustled.

Mrs. Wilkinson stood behind him, wearing a big plastic hat.  She was holding the baby, who was chewing on her sleeve.  Elsie and Junior were crowded on either side of her.

"You're welcome," Mom said. "Um . . . did you say you were bringing eggs?"

"Right here," Mr. Wilkinson said, pulling a goose out from under his arm.

"BUCKAW!" the goose said.

We all stared at it.

"Is that a . . . chicken?" Mom asked slowly.

"No, it's a goose," Mr. Wilkinson said.

My father scratched his head. "Don't geese honk?"

"QUACK," the goose said.

Junior and I both started to snicker.

"Hold on!" my mom protested. "Geese honk! They shouldn't —"

"OINK," the goose said.

"You bought that at the same place you got the apple tree, didn't you?" my father asked.

"No, the apple tree grew on its own," Mr. Wilkinson said. "Now, let's get started!"

He strode into the house, pushed aside the water and dyeing kits, and plopped the goose onto the kitchen table. The goose immediately started eating the old newspapers beneath it.

"Please tell me you don't expect that bird to lay our Easter eggs," Dad said. "You realize birds lay one egg a day. Less, usually —"

"Cluck cluck cluck cluck MEOW!" the goose cried, flaring its wings. A black egg with white writing on it thudded on the table.

My mother's mouth opened wider and wider.

"I thought it might be wise to not let Junior have dye," Mr. Wilkinson said. "Last Easter, he turned the house purple."

"That was an *accident*," Junior said. "It was supposed to be green."

"Let me try! Let me try!" my sister cried. She ran over to the goose and held out a corner of newspaper. The goose gulped it down. We all waited, with baited breath.

"Squeak squeak squeak squeak SQWACK!" the goose cried, flapping its wings wildly.

Another black egg with white writing landed on the table. I turned my head sideways, and could make out a backwards *Financial Security*.

"Can it do anything other than newspaper?" Elsie asked.

"Try," Mr. Wilkinson said, gesturing.

So Elsie looked around the table, saw the limp centerpiece of fake flowers that my mom put out every year, and plucked a small one.

She brought it over to the goose.

"Purr purr purr purr WOOF!" the goose said, flapping wildly.

*Thud.* Another egg landed on the table. This one was white with flowers all over it.

"Let me try! Let me try!" my sister cried, running over. She grabbed the plastic Minnie Mouse watch from her wrist and dangled it in front of the goose.

"Hey," Dad protested. "That might be a cheap watch, but —"

*Gulp.* "Meh meh meh meh BAAAA!"

Genevieve's eyes glittered with excitement. She held up a pink egg that seemed to be coated with plastic. On it were three painted hands that were still ticking. The skinny red second hand was still moving.

"My turn!" I shouted. I ran into the kitchen and grabbed the first thing I could find in a drawer.

"My new spatula!" Mom cried.

"Gobble gobble gobble gobble NEIGH!"

I held up my new egg in triumph. It was coated in silver metal with rings of black Teflon to decorate it.

"That spatula wasn't new," Dad said. "You've had it for five years. And never used it."

My mom was the worst cook in the universe.

"I was thinking about trying to make omelets with the leftover eggs next week," Mom said defensively.

"Thanks for saving us from that fate, Donovan," Dad said dryly.

I grinned, tossing my egg up in the air.

"Don't toss them!" Mr. Wilkinson said. "That's one of the disadvantages of doing this. Those are raw eggs."

I caught mine and looked at it speculatively.

"What if we feed it money?" Junior asked, his eyes gleaming yellow with anticipation.

"Ah," Mr. Wilkinson said. "You peeked."

"At what?" Genevieve asked.

"The instruction manual," Mr. Wilkinson said. "Eating money is what the goose is known for."

"What does it do?" I asked Junior eagerly.

"Try it and find out," he grinned.

I spun around. "Dad, can I have some money?"

"This is going to be an expensive Easter, isn't it?" he muttered, rooting around in his pocket.  He pulled out his wallet and found a one dollar bill.  "Here," he said.

I waved the dollar bill in front of the goose's beak.  "Heeeeere, goosey goosey . . ."

*Gulp!*  The goose's eyes glowed with yellow dollar signs.  It flapped its wings.

"CHING CHING CHING CHING!"

Three bright golden eggs landed on the table, one after another.  *Thud thud thud.*

"Are those . . . pure gold?" my father squeaked.

"Hmm?  No, they're gold plate," Mr. Wilkinson said.  "If you want solid gold, you'll have to feed it more money.  They're still goose eggs.  Try one."

I grabbed an egg and lifted it.  It wasn't as heavy as my spatula egg.

"Think fast!" Junior shouted, jumping up to knock off his mother's hat.

"Junior!" Mrs. Wilkinson shouted.

"Too late!"  Junior flung it at the goose, which opened its mouth and gobbled it down.  It was impressive how fast it disappeared.

"Chirp chirp chirp chirp BLEEEEAT!" the goose said.

An egg coated in yellow plastic and obviously-fake painted flowers landed on the table.

Mrs. Wilkinson glared at Junior.

"Let's feed it more money," Genevieve said excitedly.

In the end, we had thirty-six golden eggs, twelve plastic-coated eggs, and several other weird ones, like the egg with a Heinz logo from Dad feeding an empty ketchup bottle to the goose.

"Let's go outside and hide them."  Dad stretched his arms.

"Oh, no need," Mr. Wilkinson  said.  "We have a rabbit for that."

My mother stared at him.  "You . . . what?"

In response, Mr. Wilkinson piled the eggs into a basket, walked over to the back door, and opened it.  He set the basket on the ground, and a tiny, furry white hand grabbed it.

"Is that a real rabbit?!" Genevieve asked Elsie excitedly.

"Uh huh," Elsie said.  "Dad rented it and the goose for the weekend."

"How long is the . . . rabbit going to take?" Dad asked, eyeing the back door as it clicked shut.

# The Goose That Laid Golden Easter Eggs

"Oh, only a few minutes," Mr. Wilkinson said.

Junior sidled over to me. "Do you know what our sisters look like?" he whispered.

"A tree and a snowdrift," I said promptly. Brown-skinned Elsie was wearing a green dress with pink flowers, and cream-skinned Genevieve was wearing fluffy white lace.

"No, no, not that," Junior snorted. He stopped and eyed our sisters. "Okay, yeah, they do. But more importantly: they look like *targets.*"

I looked them over. A slow grin spread across my face. "We're going to be outside with raw eggs, aren't we?"

"Whoever creams each other's sister with the most wins," Junior whispered.

"Deal," I grinned, slapping his hand.

"What are you boys doing over there?" Mrs. Wilkinson asked suspiciously.

"Nothing," we chorused innocently.

The back door opened.

"Okay, everybody outside!" Mr. Wilkinson called.

Junior and I smirked and shot each other secret thumbs-up. Then we headed outside with our families for Easter egg hunting.

I found a clutch of gold eggs hidden in an empty birds' nest at the top of our pine tree, and put them in my pockets before climbing back down again. Junior discovered the ticking pink egg under the fence. My sister grabbed a golden egg from the bushes beside the house. Dad had two newspaper eggs in his basket.

"Hoot hoot hoot cooooo," the goose said, wandering around and gulping pine needles and bark, and laying tree-colored eggs. I scooped those up, too.

I waited until finding the eggs was boring, and then Junior and I caught each others' eyes. We nodded and grinned.

"Hey, Elsie!" I said. "Think fast!"

"What?" she asked, turning around.

*Splat!* I got her right in the pink sash! *Splat!* Across the front of her dress.

"DONOVAN!" she screamed.

A shrill shriek carried from the other side of the lawn. "What are you — *Mommmm!*"

Genevieve bolted past us, Junior chasing after and pelting her. "There's no escaping the golden eggs!" he shouted.

I spun around to throw some more at Elsie, but she was up the tree.

"Take that!" she shouted. "And that! And that!"

I dodged, but one of her eggs hit me. *Splat!* on my head.

"How do you like that?" she yelled, her eyes purple.

"I'm better at it than you!" I shouted back, grabbing three eggs and flinging them up at the tree.

*Splat! Splat!* Two hits! Yes! I was winning!

"THAT DOES IT!" a voice thundered across the lawn. "EVERYONE, STOP!"

We all fell to a halt.

Mr. Wilkinson stormed over to us, his eyes dark red.

*Oops,* I thought.

"What," he demanded, "did you boys think you were doing?"

Elsie slid down from the tree and folded her arms. Genevieve stormed over, dripping and glaring.

"She got you," Junior told me. "That's minus one point to you."

"My score's still higher than yours," I said.

"Was this some kind of competition?" Mr. Wilkinson demanded. "Hitting your sisters with eggs?"

I stared at him in puzzlement. "Yeah." Why did he need to ask?

"Well, you've forgotten one very important thing," Mr. Wilkinson said. He glanced down at the goose, which was chomping on the dirt and laying dirt-colored eggs.

"The fact that the goose was out here?" I asked.

"No," Mr. Wilkinson said. He reached down and scooped up the line of seven eggs that the goose had just laid. "The fact that I went to college on a baseball scholarship."

Junior and I started to back away.

"Get 'em!" Elsie cheered.

"Eggs! Eggs! Eggs!" Genevieve shouted.

"He shoots!" Mr. Wilkinson said. "He scores . . ."

Junior and I booked it across the yard.

"MOOOOO!" the goose called after us.

# I Do Not Want to Take a Nap

Emily
Martha
Sorensen

I do not want to take a nap.

I want to stay on Mommy's lap.

I do not want to go to bed.

I want to play with Dad instead.

I do not want to go to sleep.

Don't make me, or I'll cry and weep.

I do not want a turned-off light.

Don't try it, or I'll scream and fight.

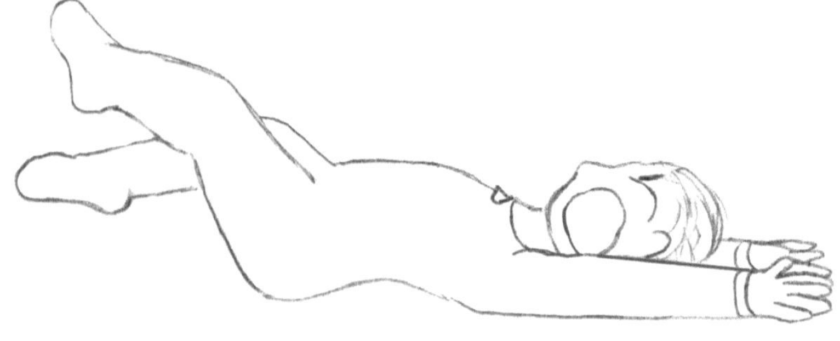

I do not want to take a nap!  I —

ZZZZZZZZZZ

# The Toddler's Lament

(This poem came first!  I chose to illustrate it later.)

- 28 -

I do not want to take a nap.
I want to stay on Mommy's lap.

I do not want to go to bed.
I want to play with Dad instead.

I do not want to go to sleep.
Don't make me, or I'll gnash and weep.

I do not want a turned-off light.
And if you try, I'll scream and fight.

I do not want to take a nap.
I zzzzzzzz

# 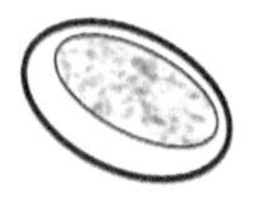 Little House in the Crater

Their faces were scrawny and pink and terrible. Their two eyes glittered. High on their heads where antennae should be, the wild humans had coarse fur.

When Laura peeked out from behind the mound, both humans were looking straight at her. Her thorax and wings trembled with fear. Two dingy-grey eyes stared down into her compound ones. The human did not move, not one of its arm segments moved. Only its eyes glinted at her. She didn't even breathe.

She heard the humans squat down by the food-pit. She heard Ma turn off the barrier. After a while she heard them eating. The humans ate all of the carrion that Ma had brought in. They ate every morsel of it. When every scrap was gone, the humans rose up. The smell was atrocious. One of them made harsh sounds in its throat. Ma looked at it with trembling eyes; she did not say anything. The humans turned and walked back through the tunnel entrance.

Ma let out a thin, keening sigh. She brushed Laura's arm in comfort as they watched the humans going away, out of the tunnel entrance.

"Never mind," Pa said. "The main thing is to be on good terms with the natives. We'll finish the extermination once we're done terraforming Earth."

# Mirror Image

It was all my reflection's fault that I got grounded for two weeks.

I woke up early on Saturday morning, and I was eager to have the whole apartment to myself while Mama and Papa were still asleep. I tiptoed past the hall mirror, thinking I could make myself some cocoa and maybe even watch cartoons before my parents started stirring.

Then a sound like tinkling glass made me spin around, heart pounding.

Lying sprawled on the ground in front of me, looking like she'd just rolled through the mirror, was . . . me.

I stared at her, mouth open.

"Who are you?!" I squeaked.

"Airam," she said, shaking her hair. It was long in the front and ragged in the back, just like mine. It had been an accidental haircut, and it was hideous. Surely nobody else in the whole world had a haircut like me.

"Maria," I said shakily. "Where — where did you come from?"

"There," she said, pointing.

I swallowed, looking in the mirror. I could see the carpet, threadbare and stained, and the wall behind me, and . . .

The wall *behind* me?

"Where's my reflection?!" I shrieked.

"Shhhhhh!" Airam looked alarmed. "If you wake up your parents, mine are going to wake up too. And I'll get in humongous trouble. It's, well, it's sort of forbidden."

"What is?" I hissed, barely believing I was doing what she said.

"Crossing through to reality." She bit her lip and looked innocent. "I've heard rumors that it's deadly . . . only it's not, is it?  Look! I'm here!  I made it safely!"

She raised her arms in a cheering position.

"You mean . . . you're my reflection?" I asked stupidly.

"Uh huh," she nodded.  Then she squealed.  "Oh, wow!  I've never seen that section of the hallway!  Nothing's ever reflecting it, so on my side it's totally empty!"

She ran down the hallway to the kitchen.  I ran after her, not sure what else to do.  She stopped abruptly, and I stumbled and fell right through her.

"The *kitchen*," she breathed.  "All we ever get are pieces that are warped and blurry.  You know, from pots and spoons and things. This is amazing."

I didn't even spare a glance at the kitchen.  It was cramped and tiny and boring.  What I couldn't believe was that I had just run *through* somebody.

"Oh," she gasped, pointing at the cereal boxes on top of the fridge.  "Can I have some?  Please, please, please?  In my world, we have no sense of taste."

With some misgivings, I fetched the stool from under the sink. Then I reached the corn flakes box, opened the top, and held it out to her.

She reached in and pulled out a translucent corn flake.  She popped it in her mouth and closed her eyes, savoring it.

"Mmmm," she said.  "I can't believe I have a real sense of taste."

"What did you do?" I blurted out.  "I've never seen a corn flake go see-through like that!"

"I can't touch solid things," she said, like it was obvious. "Here, look.  See?"

She ran her hand through the refrigerator.  My flesh crawled as it came out unscathed.

"What I ate was the image," she said happily.  "Somewhere in that box, there's now an invisible corn flake."

I looked at the box, shivering.  I didn't think I'd be eating cereal today.

"What's next?" she asked eagerly.  "Can we go outside?  I've never seen the outside, never.  I've heard, in this world, you guys play all sorts of games . . ."

I opened the window to the kitchen so that she could look out. We were up by seven stories.

"I'm not allowed to go outside without permission," I explained.

"Oh." In the bright sunlight, she looked disappointed. That and dingy. "Then what can we play?"

I frowned, squinting. Maybe it was just my imagination, but it seemed like she was starting to fade a little bit.

"Umm . . ." I said. "Are you supposed to be see-through?"

She looked down at her arm, puzzled. Then she yelped.

"*That's* what they mean when they say it's deadly! I — I think I'm disappearing!"

"Then how do we get you back?" I asked urgently. "Will you just go back if you disappear here entirely?"

She gulped. "I . . . I don't know," she said in a small voice. "I don't think so. I think I'd die for good if I disappeared here."

*Oh, great.* I pounded my forehead with my fist. That was the last thing I wanted. I got teased enough at school as it was — I didn't need to add "Ooh, she's got no reflection, she must be a vampire" on top of it.

Airam ran back to the hallway mirror.

"It got me here, so it might get me back," she called, stepping through it.

For a moment, there was silence. Then she returned through the wall, looking ashen.

"There was no image to step through," she said, quavering. "Because we're both here. I'm going to be stuck forever!"

My throat seized with panic. "What about a picture of me? Do you think that would work?"

She brightened up. "A picture," she breathed. "An image of you, just like me . . . yes, it may!"

I ran back to my bedroom and found my old school picture buried under a pile of homework from last year. "Will this do?" I panted, holding it out to her.

She reached for it, her fingers trembling.

For a moment, things seemed hopeful. She flickered, kind of like a candle flame. Then she dropped it and started wailing.

"It's too similar!" she bawled. "I won't fit! I'm never going to get back home again! I'm going to die here!"

I bit my lower lip. We had to think of something.

"We need something that's completely different," Airam said. "But what's the opposite of a reflection?"

I shook my head. "I don't know."

"Take me back to the kitchen," she said in despair. "At least I can eat one last thing before I disappear forever."

I spilled half of the cereal boxes as I got them down for her, but we didn't have time to worry about that. In the sunlight streaming from the window, she seemed more see-through than ever.

Airam gulped down handfuls of images, leaving invisible cereal strewn all over the kitchen. I sat on the stool, head in my hands, staring at the window.

What was the opposite of a reflection? Images were just light bouncing away, I knew that from science class. The opposite would absorb it.

What absorbed light? Darkness.

Where would I find a dark version of me?

I stared at the floor, which looked nearly empty because Airam was eating images so quickly. A dark shape stretched out behind me.

Wait a minute.

"Airam!" I cried. "Jump into my *shadow!*"

She stared at me for a moment, her mouth open. Then she dropped a handful of Cheerios and dove for the shape behind me.

I held my breath, waiting. There was a sound like slurping.

"WHY IS ALL THIS CEREAL ALL OVER THE FLOOR?!"

I spun around, eyes wide. Mama stood there in her bathrobe, looking furious.

I gulped. "It was my reflection," I tried to explain. "You see —"

My explanation didn't go over too well. Even after I swept the floor, Mama kept stepping on cereal, and she didn't believe me when I tried to explain half of them were invisible. In the end, because she was "sick of me lying," I ended up getting grounded for two weeks.

But it was okay. Because I had a mirror in my bedroom, and that gave me time to practice backwards writing.

*Are you real?* I wrote, holding the sign up clearly so that my reflection could see it. *It wasn't just a dream, was it?*

For a moment, there was nothing. Just my own face staring at me.

Then slowly, deliberately, Airam winked.

I smiled and wrote another sign backwards. *You'll have to come back tomorrow.*

There were worse ways to spend a grounding.

# Knock Three Times

Ellie cleaned the house because she absolutely had to.
Her stepsisters were slobs, and her stepmother was quite bad, too.
"Your standards are just way too high," her stepmother protested.
"You cleaned the grate an hour ago!" her stepsisters attested.
But Ellie couldn't help it, be it crumb or dust or hairs —
She simply had to keep perfection up and downstairs.
"It could be worse," stepmother sighed; "her father spoke rhymes.
At least she only cleans a lot, and knocks three times."

A messenger came to the house with fancy invitation
For them to all attend a three-day royal celebration.
But on the first night all of them were heading out the door,
The younger sister tripped and splashed ink all across the floor.
"Don't clean it up!" the older cried. "We shouldn't delay!"
"Then go without me!" Ellie shouted. "I have to stay!"
Her sisters waited half an hour, but she'd found new grimes.
So they left as Ellie fiercely scrubbed and knocked three times.

At last, her task completed, Ellie sat back and cried.
She'd wanted to go to the ball, and now had no ride.
The front door then burst open; her godmother barged in.
"Your whole family is worried, Ellie! Where to begin?!
It's a good thing I have magic, girl. I'll make you a coach.
Fetch me pumpkin, mice, and lizards now," she said with reproach.
Soon the pumpkin was a grand coach with the faintest of slimes.
Ellie vigorously cleaned the seats and knocked three times.

When she found the royal ballroom, all her tensions relaxed.
She had never seen a floor quite so exquisitely waxed.
She squealed about it to the prince, and he was bemused.
"Is it really that exciting?" he asked.  "Yes!" she enthused.
He found this so entertaining that they danced for hours long,
And before either had realized it, the night was half-gone.
At her curfew, she was dragged away with the midnight chimes,
With her mind so full of him . . . she didn't knock three times.

On the next night, the prince watched the door like a hungry hawk,
But she had to stay home because she'd forgotten to knock.
So her sisters dropped her shoe into the lost and found claims.
(A subtle hint because the prince was awful with names.)
The prince found it, and cried out that he wanted to date
The girl who'd worn this tiny slipper!  (It was size eight.)
Five hundred ladies claimed it theirs and other such crimes,
But none of them were her, and none knocked three times.

He went from house to house to find the girl of his dreams
(Not noticing her address had been sewn in the seams).
At last he found the right one, where her family was housed.
"It's past time; it's been weeks now," her two stepsisters groused.
"She's hiding in her bedroom now.  She's locked herself in!
She thinks you made her commit some unpardonable sin."
He stared; then they explained it all in whispers and mimes.
So he went to Ellie's door, and then he knocked three times.

There was silence for a moment, and then Ellie emerged.
Hopefully, the prince asked, "Has the problem been purged?"
Shakily, she nodded.  So he grabbed both her hands.
"In that case, do you think that we could make dinner plans?"
The stepsisters squealed loudly and clapped hands in delight.
Ellie's face was crimson and now glowing quite bright.
"I guess it's not so bad if you distract me sometimes . . ."
The prince grinned, and together, they both knocked three times.

# The Reason Why My Paper is Late

It was all because of the alien abduction.

You know how it is — I was typing on my computer, and that box came up that said: *Congratulations! You have been randomly chosen for the honor of an alien abduction! Click the "okay" button if this is acceptable to you.*

So I clicked the "okay" button, and then I was gone for a week. I don't remember anything that happened, but I have a few new scars, which is cool. Unfortunately, I think the teleporter glitched, because my paper got deleted.

Anyway, can I have an extra week to finish it?

Teacher's response: Yes, but you are reminded that students are only allowed one abduction per semester. If abducted again, please contact your overlord to complain.

# Glass Beads

The first evidence that aliens existed was a junk heap. A trashy old ship that was barely running, strapped with a broken hyperspace drive, barely afloat, dead in space.

And it wandered aimlessly into our solar system.

We didn't realize, at first, that it was a trash heap. We went ballistic trying to contact it. When we discovered it seemed to be nothing but dead in space, we prepared a mission to visit it. For political reasons, I was selected as one of the first explorers, representative of the Native American Consensus that had taken over North America after the collapse of the United States economy.

The other team members on the ship were experts in engineering, programming, sociology, and linguistics. As a mere political inclusion, I was rather ostracized during our three-month journey. Nominally I was the leader, but in practice, I was treated with the cold politeness due to one of my rank who had not earned it through expertise.

I couldn't honestly say I blamed them. I didn't really feel I had the right to be part of this mission. I had protested the appointment for that reason, but been overridden.

All things considered, I was more than glad when we reached the derelict.

As we docked, the others' excitement was palpable. Anna Lewis, our programmer, actually licked her lips.

Since that made me nervous, I uneasily stepped to the side.

"What do you think we're going to find?" Don Sanchez, our sociologist, asked nervously. He twitched, one of the many nervous tics he had acquired during this journey. "Do you think we're going to find anything worth salvaging? Do you think we're going to find corpses, or frozen live crew members? Do you think —"

"I think we're going to find whatever we're going to find," Chinue Ndiaye, our linguist, said coolly. She was cold and rational, and her dislike of Don was exceeded only by her disdain for me.

"I just hope we'll be able to salvage something," Garth O'Harris, our engineer, muttered.

"You *would* hope that, wouldn't you?" Anna snapped. "All you ever think about is what you want. You, you, you. Never mind that all the rest of us are after knowledge."

*Oh, boy.* I stepped forward to stop them. Despite my best efforts and advice, the two of them had embarked on a passionate romance a month after we'd left Earth. The fiery breakup two weeks later had caused more problems than I could count since then. I had hoped the two were getting along again . . . but . . .

"Knowledge, my foot," Garth sneered, ignoring my attempt to step between them. "We all know tech is the real reason we're here. We might *want* to talk to aliens, but we *need* an FTL drive."

Garth wasn't wrong, but that didn't stop Chinue and Don from bristling.

"Learning how to construct a hyperspace drive is just another form of knowledge," I said in my best pacifist voice. "In any case, we're here as a team. We don't have separate agendas. Right?"

None of them quite met my eye as they all muttered their separate agreements.

Internally, I sighed.

This was the problem with having a representative from each of the five Earth governments on board. On paper, it looked like the best way to keep all the governments happy. In reality, we were not the cohesive team we were meant to be.

"Let's send in the bots," I said. "They'll check for any traps or active security that might pose danger to us, then we can study the footage, see if we can glean whatever we need without going in there in person —"

"Jono, we know the plan," Chinue said coldly. "We're not fools."

*Except for you*, her tone seemed to imply.

For the millionth time on this journey, I wanted to snap that I hadn't asked to be the elected leader on board, that I'd been entered on the ballot without my consent, and that I'd tried to get out of it. But now was not the time, and it was doubtful that my saying such things would change their opinion of me.

o8

Several weeks of careful study passed before Garth came to dinner one night and announced that there was nothing more he could study from a distance, and that he wanted to be the first to enter the alien ship himself tomorrow.

Anna, predictably, disagreed vehemently. "I haven't even deciphered half of their machine language yet, and I'm not even certain it *does* use trinary. You could easily walk into a death trap, and I'd have no way to disarm it remotely."

Garth was not swayed. "We're heading back to Earth in eight days, and we haven't got the fuel to tow the whole thing with us. I've got to figure out what parts we want to take back."

"That's why we have *bots!*" Anna snapped.

Garth shook his head. "Those things are just too clumsy. They weren't designed to undo those weird bolts the aliens used. Some of the stuff they've brought me has wound up scratched or mangled. I'm not gonna trust them with something as important and potentially fiddly as the hyperspace drive."

"I want to go, too," Chinue spoke up.

I blinked and stared at her in surprise.

"What could you want to do there?" Garth scoffed. "You can do your language-deciphering just fine from the video feeds."

"Sometimes it helps to be physically present," Chinue said coolly. "It helps one gain a better understanding of cultural context."

"In that case, I should go, too," Don said quickly, snatching up the food packet that Chinue was reaching for. She gave him a look of disgust. He ripped his open, his head twitching to the side slightly in one of his many tics, and said, "Culture is exactly what I'm here to study."

*Oh, great.* It dawned on me what was actually going on here. None of them wanted the member of another nation to be the first on board the ship.

Anna caught on a split second after I did.

"I'll go, too. It might be useful to me for the same reasons."

"How?" Don scoffed. His fingers jerked side to side. "You're a programmer. Their code is all the context you need."

"Not true," Anna retorted. "Examining more of their hardware might give me useful information about how they arrange their bits. And there's such a thing as social engineering. Perhaps someone left the equivalent of a password written down somewhere that wasn't covered in a video feed."

"Hang on," I said, holding up my hand. "We shouldn't all go at once. Let's try it one at a time. We can draw lots to see who goes first, if necessary."

All four of them stared at me with contempt.

"Then you stay behind, Jono," Chinue said disdainfully.

Given that I would have nothing useful to do on board, and the risks were certainly non-zero, that was exactly what I'd planned on doing. But seeing those four sets of eyes staring at me, I had the crushing realization that I couldn't afford to do that.

If my four supposed allies discovered anything Earth-changing on that ship, they might very well cut me out of it. And if the Native American Consensus got cut out of a possible technological revolution, my bosses' reaction would not be pretty.

Not to mention the voters. I might not like this job, but I really wanted the chance to run for an office I *did* want in the future.

And so, unfortunately, unwise as it might be for all of us to go in at once, if the others were insisting on it, I couldn't afford to be left behind.

"Well, then we'll all go in together," I said calmly.

I kept my voice completely level, even though I really wanted to snap at them all to please, for once, just think like a team.

8

At first, everything seemed exactly as expected from the bots' video feeds. We proceeded with caution, one at a time, drawing straws at every turn to see who walked in front. That person would take the greatest risk and also potentially have a slight advantage in seeing interesting things before everyone else.

Ten straw-drawing rotations later, we'd had no surprises.

"Bots got all the traps, I think," Anna said.

"Bots didn't find any traps," Garth returned.

"None at all?"  Anna looked troubled.  "You'd think there'd be some kind of security."

"Must be a very trusting species," Chinue opined.

"Or this whole place is a trap," Don muttered.

I didn't add my opinion, but I was more than glad when Garth drew the short straw next.

We reached the back of the ship, where the hyperspace drive was waiting, without incident.  Garth got down on his hands and knees and opened a bag slung across his shoulder full of twisting and prying tools.  Nobody interfered, or even spoke.  We all just stood there and watched as he screwed, pried, chipped, and finally wrenched the first bolt loose.

The ship around us shook, and we tumbled sideways or grabbed walls for support.

An unfamiliar, gruff, robotic voice spoke out of thin air:

"THIS IS OUR SHIP."

There was a sharp intake of breath from Anna, and Don's eyes widened.  Chinue got up from the floor, expressionless as she stood.

"I'm pleased to meet you," she said.  "It seems you speak English."

There was a slight rattling, and the voice said:

"YES.  DO YOU WANT THIS SHIP?"

*Straight to the point*, I realized.  I opened my mouth to answer.

"Why are you asking?" Chinue said.

That was exactly what I'd been about to say, so I shut my mouth and let her handle it.  Officially, she was supposed to be in charge of any communication with aliens if the opportunity happened.  Granted, this was because the assumption had been that we'd have to figure out their language and she'd be the most skilled at it.

"IF YOU WANT THIS SHIP, WE ARE WILLING TO NEGOTIATE."

I let out a low whistle.  Garth crouched in place, his hands frozen as we waited.

Chinue thought for a moment.  Then she said carefully, "We want ownership of this ship, all parts of it we have brought on board our own vessel, all the records we have made about it, and the right to use this ship or any knowledge that we might gain from it in any way we wish."

"AGREED," the voice said with no hesitance. "AND WE WILL HAVE JUPITER."

Chinue looked taken aback. "Jupiter?" she repeated. "You mean the gas giant in our solar system?"

"YES. YOU WILL HAVE THE SHIP, AND WE WILL HAVE JUPITER."

"Very we—" Chinue started to say.

"Are you crazy?!" I broke in. "Excuse me, alien race, whoever we're speaking with, the person you have been talking to does not have the authority to speak for our species in this matter. It must be brought before the Earth governments, and the leaders of our species will make the negotiations."

There was silence for a long moment.

"YOU HAVE ALREADY TAKEN PARTS OF OUR SHIP. YOU HAVE RECORDS. IF WE CANNOT MAKE A DEAL, THOSE PIECES MUST BE RETURNED, AND THOSE RECORDS MUST BE DESTROYED."

I swallowed. It would be awful to go home empty-handed, but far better that than to make a rash deal that our species might regret later. "We would be willing to surrender those records to you —"

"SOME OF THOSE RECORDS ARE IN YOUR BRAINS. IF WE CANNOT MAKE A DEAL, YOU MUST ALSO BE DESTROYED."

A chill shot down my spine.

"Jono," Chinue whispered to me, "I'm not an idiot. I know what they want is probably worth more than what we'll get. But think about our differences in technology. They could just exterminate our whole species and take what they want anyway."

"We're not planning to use Jupiter for anything," Anna said, her voice shaking slightly. "Let them have it."

"We're not in a good negotiating position," Don agreed.

"Two words," I told them. *"Glass beads."*

Chinue stared at me in incomprehension, but behind her, I saw understanding dawn in Don's eyes.

"We need the hyperspace drive," Garth insisted.

"We need a *working* hyperspace drive," I returned. "Aliens: we would be willing to sell you the planet Jupiter in exchange for a working hyperspace drive, full instructions on how to use it, a working ship to use it on, and the right to build more."

There was silence for a very long moment.

"NO DEAL."

Anna's arms tensed.  Garth looked like he wanted to scream at me.  Chinue's icy glare seemed to have come from the depths of the Arctic.

"Isle of Manhattan?" Don asked me, stepping forward.

I nodded.

"Would you please explain what you mean?" Anna snapped.

"Later," I said.  Explaining it here right in front of our audience seemed most unwise.

"Aliens," Don said, raising his voice.  "We will agree to *lease* you the planet of Jupiter for one year, with a clause for that lease to be renewed by Earth's governments under whatever terms you and they mutually agree on.  In exchange, whatever knowledge we have gained from this ship will be ours to keep.  We will return any pieces of the ship that we have removed, and we will not take anything further from it."

There was silence for a long time.  A very, very long time.

"AGREED," the voice said.

I breathed out a deep breath I hadn't realized I'd been holding.  I felt rather faint.

"But —" Garth objected, looking at the hyperspace drive he'd been trying to get at.

"We leave now," I said, my voice sharp.  "We leave with our lives.  We leave our governments in the best negotiating position possible."

"But we need —"

"*NOW!*" I roared.

For the first time since leaving Earth, all four of my team members listened to me.

We beat a hasty retreat.

08

"So what were you talking about?" Anna asked twelve hours later.  We were all seated around the table.  "What did glass have to do with it?"

We had sent our bots to return everything we had removed from the other ship and taken off to return to Earth as quickly as possible.  It was only now, with the ship at least eight hours behind us, that I no longer felt jumpy fearing that the aliens were listening in on every word we might say.

I looked over at Don. "Do you want to explain?"

He shrugged. "It probably hits closer to home for you. You explain."

I took a deep breath. "There's a story that the Isle of Manhattan was bought from the Native American tribe who owned it for a handful of glass beads. It's not historically accurate, but it's not all that far off, either. The term is often used in bureaucratic circles in the Native American Consensus as shorthand for, 'Make sure you understand the value of what you're trading away.'"

There was silence around the table.

"You think Jupiter's that valuable?" Anna asked.

"An entire planet?" I asked. "Undoubtedly."

"But we don't have any plans to use it," Garth said. "And we need a hyperspace drive!"

"It wasn't a real hyperspace drive," I said, shaking my head. "Think about it. The aliens waited as long as possible to contact us. That was smart, because it strengthened their negotiating position. The more we learned, the more excuse they had to threaten to kill us if we didn't give them what they wanted. And the more we learned, the more we'd want the technological goodies they were offering. The longer they waited, the better their advantage, in other words."

"But they rushed to contact us as soon as they saw we were about to open up the hyperspace drive," Chinue said slowly.

"Which was the one thing we wanted most of all," I said, nodding. "Why would they do that? Their position would've been better if we'd studied it enough to know how desperately we wanted to keep it. Unless . . ."

Garth banged the table with both fists and put his head in his hands.

"So Don was right," Anna said. "The whole place was a trap."

"Yes," I nodded. "Just not quite the kind we expected. It was a trap to get us to sign a bad deal."

Chinue breathed out. "You realize that humanity is still not in a good negotiating position. The governments on Earth might not be able to do any better than we did."

"You're right," I conceded. "But at least the experts will have the chance to try."

*And if they decide I'm the right man for the job,* I promised myself silently, *this time I'll retire.*

# Computer Gremlins

My computer has a gremlin infestation. I know because one started talking to me.

"That was delicious," it left on one of my documents. "Syrupy poetry."

"Rather dry," it complained, gnawing on a tax file. "There's no story."

"Needs fewer adverbs," it grumbled, slurping down an e-mail.

"Ooh, tasty snack!" it added, crunching my Twitter feed.

Things got so bad that I installed anti-gremlin software. But that only seemed to encourage them. Finally, I trapped them in a neverending loop of a computer-generated document that writes "The Song That Never Ends" forever.

Now, if only *that one* would stop singing . . .

# The Dark Lord's Genie

"All right," the genie said. "No man shall ever kill you. Now, as to my payment —"

"Hey, wait a minute!" the Dark Lord protested. "What about women?"

The genie snapped his fingers. "Fine. No living human. Your bill is —"

"And what about dead ones? I've heard about poltergeists —"

"No human, living or dead, will be able to kill you!"

"Well, what about dogs?"

The genie paused. "Now you're just being annoying."

"Also, what about inanimate objects? It doesn't do me much good if 'humans' can't kill me, but a sword can . . ."

Five minutes later, the genie killed the Dark Lord.

# The Day of Shoulder Angels

I wish they'd never invented Morality Day.

"Go apologize to Helen," my shoulder angel insisted, poking my cheek.

"Go TP her house," my shoulder demon grinned, twisting my earlobe.

"Leave her a plate of cookies," the angel added, tugging my hair.

"Smash a carton of eggs on her door," the demon smirked, kicking my collarbone.

"STOP IT!" I shouted, hurling them away. "I hate both of you!"

I stormed off, and for one blissful moment, I had peace. Then . . .

"I think you should apologize to me," the angel sniffed.

"I think you should kick her off again," the demon grinned.

# Pixie Eggs

Someone
Took pixie eggs
Aboard our spaceship.
It was not a bright move.
Pixie eggs are contraband
On hyperspace starships
For intelligent reasons.
But nobody noticed
Until too late.

Stored
In a suitcase
As souvenirs of
The pixies' planet,
They were hidden
From Customs
Too well.

So when
The spaceship
Entered hyperspace,
The eggs hatched into
A swarm of pixies.
Only one thing
Could result.

Havoc!

Havoc!

Havoc!

Havoc!

Havoc!

Havoc!

Havoc!

Havoc!

# Miss Galaxy

I nearly stepped into an oozing puddle.

"Excuuuuse me!" the alien beauty queen said.

My face flushed. "Sorry."

"Now, we brought you here because of humans' reputation for unbearable ugliness," my guide said, speaking cheerfully as if my presence here were a great honor instead of an involuntary abduction. "That will make you impartial in judging our Miss Galaxy competition. Come in!"

I followed him into the giant space dome, trying to feel flattered. After all, I had been chosen above all the humans on Earth. But it was pretty hard.

After all, back home, *I* had been Miss Galaxy.

# Way Too Familiar

("The Body-Borrower" predates this.)

"Have you been borrowing my body again?" Tasha demanded, glaring at the dog.

Woofie looked at her with huge, angelic eyes, as if to say *Who, me?*

Tasha held out her hands. "There are dog biscuit crumbs all over these! Who said that you could use my body when I'm practicing astral projecting?"

Woofie panted and thumped her tail.

Tasha shook her head in annoyance.

*Highly magical!* the salesman had said. *Can act as a companion and a spell enhancer!*

What he had conveniently failed to mention was that pets were still pets.

She should never have gotten a familiar.

# Standardized Testing

Miss Hatkinson wandered between rows, avoided tripping on the dinosaur-centaur's tail, and nudged the cords of an air machine away from the walkway as she passed a methane-breathing squidlike student.

Two fuzzy aliens in the front row started giggling uncontrollably. Miss Hatkinson's eyes narrowed in suspicion.

She turned back to the air machine and searched the cords until she found the tiny box she was looking for.

"This is a brain-booster!" she scolded, holding it up. "Do you think I don't know that your species performs better when you listen to ultrasonic frequencies?" She slammed it on the table. "Cheating!"

Supervising standardized tests was a nightmare on this starbase.

#  The Silent Princess

Selenna stood on her tiptoes, staring with anguish down into the moat. She hadn't meant to toss her golden ball down there. It was a family heirloom. What was she going to do?

A bubble of slime burst from the water, and a frog sprang up. It gestured wildly at the bottom of the moat.

Selenna squinted, trying to figure out what it was doing. Was it saying it could get the ball for her? Hopefully, she nodded.

The frog plopped down into the wet, stinky hole. She watched with baited breath. A moment later, it reappeared, clutching her golden ball in its slippery hands.

Hurray! Selenna beamed and grabbed it. Then she fled back to the castle.

Only two hours later, Selenna was savoring dinner when she saw her father jump, as if startled. A footman kicked the door open and carried that frog in.

Selenna smiled and waved. The frog turned its back and hopped over to her father. There were several long minutes of waved arms and mouth movements. Bored, Selenna helped herself to an extra roll from the platter and spread jelly on it.

She stopped when she felt her father's hand on hers. She looked up. He slid a piece of paper over to her.

*Did you make this frog promises you didn't keep?* it said.

Selenna stared at that in bafflement. Promises? What was he talking about?

*No,* she wrote, confused.

The king scratched his beard, looking uncertain. Then he wrote, *The frog is claiming you promised to love him, and let him eat from your plate, and let him sleep in your bed. Did you?*

*NO!* she wrote indignantly.

The king rubbed his forehead. He went back over to the frog. Their mouths moved for a long time, and their arms were waving back and forth. Selenna squinted, trying to figure out what the problem was.

Her father stomped back, and slid another piece of paper at her.

*The frog claims you made the bargain with him. He is calling on the ancient laws of hospitality. He claims it does not matter if you did not understand. I think we have to do what he says.*

Selenna's mouth opened in indignation. She glared at him. She grabbed the first paper he'd written on, and jabbed *eat from your plate* and *sleep in your bed* over and over again, shaking her head vehemently.

The king looked weary. He took his second note and underlined *the ancient laws of hospitality* and *have to do what he says.*

Selenna glared in fury.

The frog was revolting. It left slime all over everything it touched, and she kept finding bits of fly in her jam and potatoes. At last, Selenna resorted to skipping dinner, resolving to wake up early and sneak a huge breakfast alone.

Letting it sleep in her bed was even worse. When she woke up, the creature had left damp slime all over her pillow. Furious, she scrubbed her hair for two hours in the bathtub. Some things were more important than breakfast.

When she came out, the frog leapt in the air and attached itself to her face. That was the last straw! She wrenched it off her chin and flung it at the wall in fury.

As soon as it hit the wall, the frog transformed into a human man. Selenna blinked, confused and rather frightened. What in the world . . .?

The man waved his arms and moved his mouth, taking a deep bow in an extremely pompous way. Selenna grabbed her pillow and threw it right in his face.

It knocked him over.  He fell down and rubbed his head.  He glared at her, then hunted around for a piece of paper.  He found a pile by the door, retrieved the quill, and scribbled something on the top piece.  Then he tossed it to her.

Keeping one eye on the suspicious individual, Selenna read it.

*I'm a prince*, it said.  *A cruel fairy enchanted me.  By fulfilling the terms of the bargain, you set me free.  But you also have to love me, or I'll revert to a frog again.  Will you consent to marry me?*

Selenna read this note, then reread it.  She stared at it incredulously.  Then she snatched the quill and wrote on the other side.

*If you wanted me to love you, you should have acted with manners.  Of course not!  Are you out of your mind?*

She shoved it in his face until he'd read it.  His eyes widened with horror as his skin began to melt.  A moment later, he was a slimy frog again.

Selenna picked it up by the leg and dropped it out the window, into the moat.

# Dragon Bait

They left her as bait for the dragon.  It only made sense: She'd been a stranger on the road, and none of the villagers wanted to sacrifice their own daughters.

As the dragon swooped down, wings spread, she raised her head and shouted in a strange tongue.  The dragon stopped, looking confused.

*What those fools didn't realize,* she thought, stripping the chains off her arms and legs, *was that no innocent girl would walk alone on the roads like that.  Only a witch would dare.*

"Come on now," she crooned to her new pet.  "Let's go destroy that village together."

# Easy Target

Alfon eyed the street, watching for a target to rob. He was hungry, and the only way to get dinner was to steal something worth fencing.

A tottering old man with a tall cane caught his eye. His clothes were shabby, his beard straggly, his eyes unfocused. Perfect.

Alfon dove forward and seized the cane, which was covered in intricate designs. He made it ten feet before lightning arced and he fell flat on the ground.

"You know," the old man said distantly, wandering over to pluck it up, "most thieves have better sense than to steal a wizard's staff."

# The Librarian is In

"I just want this map so I can go on my quest!"

"And I'm telling you that you don't have a library card," the librarian scolded.

"Fine!" the paladin said in exasperation. "What would it take to get one?"

"Proof of quest, prophecy, and party role," she said.

Annoyed, the paladin pulled out his wallet and shoved over the documents. In his father's day, no governments required ID. But now . . .

"You're all set," the librarian said.

The paladin slammed the map down on the table. "Great. I'd like to check this out."

"That's from the reference section," the librarian said.

# One Midsummer's Night

One midsummer's night
With a moon you could see,
The wild fairies came
To take something from me.

They offered me beauty.
I said, "I don't need it."
They offered me wisdom.
I said, "I won't cede it."

They offered me power.
I said, "Don't need ranks."
They offered me humor.
I said, "Nah, no thanks."

They offered me friendship.
I said, "Are you crazy?"
They offered me money.
I said, "That's just lazy."

They offered me magic.
I said, "Still no way."
They offered a pet dragon.
Hmm . . .

# The Body-Borrower

Tasha opened her eyes to see the kitchen ceiling. She blinked, as this wasn't where she'd left from. She was lying flat on her back on the kitchen floor, instead of in her bed.

She looked suspiciously over at the room's other occupant.

"Angel," she growled, "have you been borrowing my body again?"

The large, shaggy puppy pawed the ground innocently.

"Are you trying to get caught?" Tasha demanded. "You know Mom's trying to breed a familiar. You know you don't belong in this world. And you're the one who begged me to not let her find out!"

Angel whimpered and put her paws over her eyes.

Dogs were impossible to reason with. Tasha got up off the floor and muttered to herself. She was covered in doggie biscuit crumbs, which were kept on the highest shelf so Angel couldn't reach them. There were also lots of dangling loops in her sweater, so probably the puppy had been pulling on them excitedly with her fingers.

"Look," Tasha said sternly. "Let's review the ground rules again . . ."

"— the opportunity of a lifetime!" Sorkan Rena's voice trilled through the front door. There was a hubbub of voices following after her. "I've got a litter of brand new kittens that will just — oh, hello, Tasha darling . . ."

Tasha nodded at her mother and the gaggle of excitable women following after her. Her mother was a charlatan of a witch, but that didn't stop other wannabes from hanging on her every word and traipsing through the house every day. None of them actually had magic, but they were all hoping that would somehow change.

# The Body-Borrower

Tasha had magic, unlike her mother.  They came from a long line of witches, but magic often skipped a generation or two.  Sometimes she thought her mother envied her more than she loved her.  And it wasn't even like magic was fun all the time.  Magic homework on top of normal homework took so much time out of her days.

No real witches came near the specialty pet shop her mother ran out of the basement, but the wannabes often bought pets from her.  There was one woman who Tasha knew for a fact now had fourteen parakeets, five piranhas, and four cats.  How she kept the cats from eating the fish and the birds was a mystery.

Tasha's mother kept hoping to capture a real familiar so that she could start breeding them, since magic ran in animal families as well as human ones.  But familiars tended to be wily and prefer their freedom to being somebody's pet, particularly a human who had no magic of their own and wanted to have a familiar for the purpose of borrowing theirs.

So the closest Tasha's mother had ever come to breeding a real familiar was one annoying tomcat who could sneak out of any cage.  Which, cats being cats, proved nothing.

The gaggle of wannabes headed downstairs, and Tasha heard their excited giggles rising up from the basement.

"Ooh, what kind is that?  I love those markings!"

"Is this the one that's always escaping from its cage?"

"Do you have lovebirds?"

"Ohhh, did you stop carrying piranhas?"

"Ouch!  That cat clawed me!"

Tasha snickered and looped her finger through Angel's collar.  The constantly-escaping-cat wasn't fond of the wannabes.

"C'mon, puppy," she said, leading the dog upstairs.

A shriek of excitement came from the basement, and a bidding war started between two gullible women.  It seemed Sorkan Rena was trying to pass off exotic lizards as baby dragons again.

Angel's tail wagged, and an excited image of chasing kittens popped into Tasha's head.

"No," she said sternly.

She settled down on her bed, lying on her stomach, and tried to concentrate on her homework.  The yells and squeals from downstairs were familiar by now.  After the "baby dragons" were sold, there would be the trained birds.  Then the dogs, then the cats.

And at the very end, for wannabes who hadn't yet bought anything, there would be the rodents. Sorkan Rena never mentioned that she didn't even try to breed them for magic, and in fact used them as cat feed.

Angel placed her drooly jowls on the back of Tasha's knee and whined. Wistful images appeared of an idealized forest scene. There were three siblings who smelled like mischief, and one runt always whimpering. There was the strong scent of fatherly protection, and the warm taste of motherly fur. Home. Warm. Love.

Tasha yelped and yanked her leg away from the dog drool.

"Angel!" she hissed. "I know you want to go home. But I don't know how to get you there! I'm sorry, but until you can explain exactly where the portal is, you're stuck here!"

Angel whined and looked at her with pitiful eyes.

"Don't look at me like that," Tasha said with annoyance. "Do you know how hard it was to convince Mom to let me keep you as my own pet? Hard! Do you know how much work I had to do to make sure you flunked every magical test she put you through? Lots! And then I had to promise that I'd take you as my only birthday present, even though I knew you'd be leaving as soon as possible anyway!"

Angel's toes pawed the ground. She whimpered.

"I know, I know," Tasha sighed. "I want to help you find your family. But I don't know how you got to this world, either. If we can just find the entrance . . ."

Her voice trailed off. They'd been searching everywhere in the neighborhood for weeks. So far, no dice. She was beginning to wonder how far Angel had wandered since crossing into this world.

At least one thing was sure: the portal couldn't just close. Once someone went through a portal one way, it wouldn't close unless that person or animal went back through it again. Or died.

It was a fact of portals that was either incredibly convenient or incredibly annoying, depending on who you asked. Personally, Tasha was glad of it right now, though when she was a fully licensed witch and had the authorization to make portals to go out and gather things like dragons' toenails, well, then she might not be so glad about the fact that the wide-open portal could let things like wyverns or dire wolves into her house. Especially since you couldn't close a portal until all of the animals had been sent back through.

For right now, though, it was a good thing.

"Tasha!" her mother called from downstairs. "I need some feed for the dragons!"

Tasha groaned and heaved herself off her bed. That was code for "these ladies aren't as gullible as I thought, and they want to see the lizards breathe fire." Since Sorkan Rena couldn't conjure anything, that meant it fell to Tasha to be her accomplice and conjure the fire and pretend the lizards were breathing it.

Angel tried to follow her down the stairs.

"No," Tasha said sternly. "You stay up here. I don't want you anywhere near Mom's pet shop. We barely got you out of there in the first place."

Angel whined and showed the image of the forest scene again.

"I *know*," Tasha said. "We'll look for it after I'm done helping Mom and I'm done doing my homework, okay?"

Angel howled and scratched at the carpet.

Tasha shut the door to her bedroom firmly. She hoped the puppy wouldn't be stupid enough to unlock it and go downstairs. Or smart enough, as the case may be.

She headed down to the kitchen, opened the door that led to the basement, and went down the second flight of stairs.

"Okay, here I am," Tasha said in a flat voice, pushing through the crowd to get to her mother, who was standing in front of the wall of exotic lizard cages. "We can get started now."

"What do you mean, 'get started'?" one of women demanded. "I thought you were getting feed for the dragons!"

Sorkan Rena gave her daughter an evil eye. "The fireflies, Tasha. From the back room."

Tasha nearly let out an audible groan. *You mean you want me to make it look like they're flying around catching those? You know I've barely started on my air conjuring lessons! I told you I wasn't ready to do that trick in public yet! In fact, I don't want to do it at all!*

But she could hardly make that objection when the audience was standing right there. The last time she had refused to help Mom in one of these demonstrations, she hadn't been given her allowance for a month. She needed her allowance.

Since she'd agreed that Angel could be her only birthday present, she hadn't been able to ask for the six music albums she actually wanted, which meant she was going to have to save up her own money to get them. Now was not a time to irritate Mom.

"Sorry," Tasha said. "I'll get the fireflies."

She squeezed back through the crowd and unlocked the doorknob to the storeroom behind the stairs with a wave of her hand. There was a soft "ooh" from one of the wannabes.

*You really shouldn't be so impressed with a simple keylock spell,* Tasha grumbled to herself. *It's not like I'm unlocking someone's car that they're trying to keep me out of. This lock was made for that spell. Even Mom can unlock it with an amulet.*

That was one of the ways Sorkan Rena pretended she was a real witch: she owned dozens of amulets. They were difficult to make and therefore expensive to buy, and could only ever be used for a single spell, though they could be used for that same spell over and over again. Tasha could understand why her mother wanted to use magic so badly, but couldn't she have a cheaper hobby and increase her daughter's allowance instead?

Or maybe even run a normal pet shop, instead of pretending she had magical animals and selling them at a premium.

But no. She knew the real reason her mother did it. Sorkan Rena wanted a familiar *herself,* so that she could use its magic to do whatever spells she wanted whenever she felt like it. And as long as that was the case, her mother was never going to stop this magical pet shop thing. Heck, she probably wouldn't stop even then. If she finally did succeed in breeding a familiar, that would only make her see dollar signs and keep on going. Real familiars would mean attracting better clientele, actual witches, who would pay a lot more than the gullible wannabes.

Inside the storeroom was the usual assortment of cans of dog and cat food, boxes of dead insects for the lizards, and stinky cages of rodents that were used as treats for the kitties.

She found the terrarium full of glowflies, fetched a net and a portable container, and then paused.

*Well, I need more practice, anyway.*

She shrugged and waved her finger to create a small whirlwind. Twirling her finger back and forth to keep it going, she opened the terrarium a crack with her other hand, and swooshed the whirlwind close enough to the top to catch five of the fireflies in it. She dropped the lid before any more could escape and tossed the net to the side, where it thumped against a tall, curtained thing. There was a slurping, sucking sound from behind the curtain, and then it fell still.

"I brought the fireflies," Tasha said, heading out of the storeroom with her hands cupped. "You can release the dragons."

As Tasha could have predicted, the trick did not go as planned. The lizards scrambled desperately through midair, seeming intensely uncomfortable, and didn't even try to catch the fireflies that zoomed across the room in panic as Tasha whooshed the petrified predators after them.

Seeing the restlessness of the women, Sorkan Rena put a stop to the trick in just under ten seconds. "Thanks, Tasha. That'll be it. Why don't you hand the fireflies to them?"

*It's about time*, Tasha thought, swatting a firefly and catching a lizard out of the air. The frantic lizard wasn't wild about eating, but she managed to shove a bug into its mouth anyway.

"AAAAAAAAAAAAH!" two women screamed as fire burst out of the lizard's mouth as soon as she removed her fingers.

Tasha smirked to herself. *Now, see, that trick I can do.*

Her mother sold two of the confused lizards to excited women, and three more bought fluffy kittens by the time the presentation ended. No dogs or birds sold this time, and the rodents didn't interest anybody, but still, five animals in one day was a pretty good number. And three more women bought overpriced magical equipment for animals they'd purchased weeks earlier, supposedly to help their familiar skills develop.

"I hope this one will be the key," one of the women said anxiously as Sorkan Rena wrapped a scratching post for her. "Fluffy doesn't seem to trust me enough to let me use his magic yet. He never even seems to notice me!"

"Familiars are notoriously difficult to get to trust you enough," Sorkan Rena said, smiling. "And even then, compatibility with their magic is never guaranteed. It's normal for it to take years for a bond to develop sometimes. But he comes from a good bloodline. It's worth keeping on trying."

"Thank you," the woman said, bobbing her head in relief. "I will."

It was all Tasha could do to keep from groaning. All that was true, which was part of the reason why familiar sales weren't regulated. Getting one that was both compatible and willing to let you use its magic if you weren't a witch was tricky. But still, her mother knew *perfectly well* that none of her animals had magical pedigrees. True, one of them could turn out to be magical, but it wasn't very likely.

Once the final customer left the store, Tasha summoned a broom from the corner and started to sweep up an avalanche of kitty litter that had spilled from a box. The constantly-escaping-tom's mischievous fault again, no doubt.

"That's enough, Tasha," her mother said, taking the broom from her hands. "You go do your homework. I will handle the rest."

Tasha looked at her queryingly. Her mother usually loved it when she helped in the store.

"I have a new amulet," her mother explained. "I want to practice with it."

Tasha barely restrained herself from asking how much it cost. *Please tell me you have enough left to pay my allowance this week.*

"What does it do?" she asked instead.

Her mother smiled mysteriously. "That's for me to know, and you to wonder about. Let's just say it's something you ought to be practicing yourself right now."

Which meant air summoning, astral projection, or silence chants, one of the things she was currently studying with her magic tutor. Probably air summoning, since it was the most exciting, and Tasha had done such a horrible job of performing with the lizards. Well, if it meant Sorkan Rena could make the lizards fly around the room by herself next time, she was welcome to it.

Tasha went upstairs, then up the next flight of stairs, and entered her bedroom to find the puppy worrying the bottom ruffle of her bedspread.

"Hey!" she complained.

Angel immediately scrambled under the bed and hid there.

Tasha sighed and flopped on top of her bed. *Homework . . . homework . . . have to do homework . . .*

Well, she'd more or less practiced enough air summoning today, and it was hard to get motivated to do normal homework, given that she'd been interrupted in the middle of math. She could do silence chants, but . . .

Tasha grinned sneakily. *Or I could use astral projection and watch Mom try out her new amulet downstairs.*

That was technically doing her homework, even though she'd already practiced astral projection today. Of course, there was one thing that she definitely had to make sure of before she did it again. Angel, the pest, had to behave.

Tasha slid off the bed and gave her sternest glare to the puppy under the bed. "No borrowing my body while I'm astral projecting this time. Got it?"

Angel wagged her tail and barked excitedly.

She wasn't sure if the puppy had actually understood her, since communication between them could be extremely fuzzy at best, but she hoped the dog had agreed.

Tasha lay down on her bed, facing upward, and put her hands on her stomach. She closed her eyes and lifted up out of her body.

It was a weird feeling, being separated from her body, but she was getting used to it. Astral travel was useful for many reasons, not the least of which being able to go through portals that were too small for your body to fit . . . or to sneak downstairs to spy on someone who thought you were doing your homework and didn't have astral sight because she wasn't a witch.

Tasha grinned.

She slipped through the floor, and then down through the floor again. Now she was back in the pet shop, but her mother was nowhere to be seen. Where . . .?

Oh, probably in the storeroom. She couldn't do magic in this form, but that was all right, because she could just walk through the door anyway. She floated through it . . .

Tasha stared at the sight before her, not believing her eyes.

Sorkan Rena lay on the ground with her hands clasped over her stomach, in exactly the same position Tasha had just left her body. Off to the side, the curtain had been pulled away, uncovering a glowing swirl of light near the floor about half a foot wide, just big enough for a puppy to fit.

*A portal!* Tasha would have gasped if she'd currently had breath to gasp with. *Is that THE portal?*

Her mind raced. It would make perfect sense. She'd always assumed her mother had found Angel wandering around outside, but maybe she hadn't. Maybe she'd hired a witch to create a portal in their basement, in the hopes that something magical would sneak through. It wasn't exactly legal to create portals without filling out the appropriate paperwork, but her mother lived sort of on the edge of the law, anyway. It would be just like her mother to think that a creature from another world would be a better shortcut to breeding familiars, even though most otherworld animals weren't magical.

*Which means she lucked out with Angel.* Tasha tried to swallow. *Which means she'll know if Angel goes through, because the portal will close. Which means she'll hire someone else to open another one, probably paying a lot of money to do so.*

Sudden misgivings rose. Spying on her mother had seemed so funny before, but now it seemed dangerous. The new amulet Sorkan Rena had bought had to give her an astral projection power. If she was astral projecting right now, she was probably on the other side of that portal. And if she came back, she would see Tasha, because she'd have astral eyes.

Tasha turned to leave, but she was too late. Her mother was already coming through the portal.

Sorkan Rena caught sight of her, and immediately did a double take. Then she rolled her eyes heavenward and disappeared into her body.

"Spying on me was not what I meant when I said to do your homework, Tasha," she said, opening her eyes. "But all right, you can help me. Come downstairs."

Feeling sheepish, Tasha rose up through the ceiling, then up through the ceiling to the next floor. She went to her bedroom, and —

Oh, for crying out loud! Where was her body *now?*

*This was not the best time to steal it, Angel!* she fumed.

She hurried to the kitchen, and sure enough, there was her body, rummaging through a box of doggie biscuits and putting one in its mouth to bite on it. Tasha's body wagged its rear end excitedly.

Tasha put her astral hands on her hips and glared at the dog.

Tasha's body beamed and wagged its rear end further.

Tasha tried to shove the puppy's astral form out of her body, but the dog was being stubborn. She could have forced the issue, but she knew from astral lessons that shoving someone out of your body could hurt them, so it was better not to do it unless they were actually an invader, as opposed to a friend pulling a dumb prank.

*Well, all right. Let's see how you like it!*

Tasha whooshed upstairs and found Angel's empty body hiding under her bed. The disobedient puppy must have taken her body the instant she'd left it.

She dove in, and immediately everything looked huge around her. Crawling out from under the bed, Tasha jogged out the door and down the stairs with tiny puppy legs.

# The Body-Borrower

She found Angel now chewing on another doggie biscuit and tugging the loops on her sweater with great entertainment.

Tasha barked in annoyance.

"For crying out loud, what's taking so long?" Sorkan Rena called, coming up from the basement. The door opened. "Tasha, come on. You're going to help."

Angel stared at her enemy with wide, frozen eyes. In Tasha's body, she let out a small whimper.

"It's not going to be *that* much work," Sorkan Rena said, shaking her head in exasperation. "I just need you to help me find some animals on the other side that can see us in astral form. That will mean they have astral sight, which will mean they have magic, which will mean they'll be workable as familiars. If we give them a good scare, we can get them to go running towards the portal, and hopefully through it."

*So that's what she's planning*, Tasha thought. She had to admit, it was a good plan. Kind of mean to the animals, but it was no worse than, say, hunting, and that was legal. The only thing was, she had promised to get Angel back home. And if she did that, the illegal portal would close, and her mother would have to pay someone a bundle to open another one.

Putting her mother in a crabby mood was something Tasha was willing to do, for Angel's sake. But how was she going to pull it off in the first place? There was no way Sorkan Rena would cooperate, and if she dragged Angel-in-Tasha's-body downstairs, and the puppy saw the portal . . . there was no telling what Angel would do. She definitely wouldn't do anything as smart as waiting patiently till she and Tasha could sneak down there tonight.

"Come on," Sorkan Rena said, taking Tasha's body's arm.

The puppy yelped, and Tasha's body collapsed.

"Tasha?" her mother asked in alarm.

*Finally!* Tasha yanked out of the puppy's body and dove into her own. As she did, she caught sight of the puppy scurrying to hide behind the pantry door.

"I . . . I'm fine," Tasha said, scrambling up to her feet. "I just — slipped for a moment. Yeah. Let's go get started . . ."

"You didn't slip," Sorkan Rena said. "That was more like . . ."

She paused.

Tasha swallowed.

". . . more like an astral form leaving," she said slowly. "And the whimpering beforehand . . . and not talking . . ."

*Darn it darn it darn it!*

"Where's that dog?"

"Angel doesn't have magic," Tasha said desperately. "I was just, like . . . pretending to be Angel. Like, for a game. It's fine."

"Mm-hmm," her mother said, her eyes narrowed, not buying it for a second. "Have you been sheltering that dog this whole time?"

"Um, no?" Tasha said desperately. "She's just a stray. You found her outside somewhere, right?"

"Wrong," Sorkan Rena said. "She came through that portal. I had high hopes that meant she'd be magical, since magical beings are better at finding portals than non-magical ones. I see all my hopes were well-founded, and I was just being lied to this whole time."

Her voice was testy.

"Mom, she wants to go home," Tasha said desperately. "I promised her she could. We can bring other animals through first, so the portal will stay open in the future, but we have to send her back afterwards. I promised."

"Go home?" Sorkan Rena said indignantly. "There's no question of that! You know how hard I've worked and how important this is. She can go back through the portal in astral form, but only once she'd been trained to find magical animals and drive them to us. As a dog, she'd be ideal to chase us cats or rabbits or rodents."

Tasha's heart plummeted. "But — but if you want to do that, the only way to keep her from jumping straight into the portal at the first opportunity —"

"— is a cage," Sorkan Rena said, nodding briskly. "Yes, she'll have to be in a cage. I'd say I'm sorry to take your pet away, but honestly, Tasha, you shouldn't have lied to me about this in the first place. I'm really very disappointed in you."

*What am I going to do?* Tasha thought frantically. *She'll make sure the cage is locked in some way that I can't unlock it — Angel will be in a cage for the rest of her life — she'll never get to go home to stay —*

An idea hit her.

Tasha flung the box of doggie biscuits that was still in her hand at the table, let out a howl to make it sound like she was sobbing, and wrenched away from her mother and ran to the living room. She ducked down into a crouched position, her face hidden in her knees.

Then she bolted out of her body and ran to where Angel was hiding in the pantry, trying desperately to climb the bottom shelf, which was too high up for her tiny body.

"Tasha?" her mother called, storming over to the living room. "Tasha! Throwing a fit does no good. I know you're disappointed, but —"

Tasha swiped her hand at Angel's face, trying to get her to take the hint. The puppy panted and wagged her tail, not getting the hint at all.

*Oh, come on! You borrow my body whenever I DON'T want you to!*

Tasha waved her hands and gestured at the box of doggie biscuits that was lying on top of the table. She waved her hand through the door to show that she was astral right now.

Angel stared at her, head cocked to the side.

*Come ON, you dumb dog!* Tasha thought, waving her hand through the door. *Get it!*

Her mother's voice continued lecturing, but it was not going to last much longer. She was going to notice Tasha wasn't moving.

Then Tasha realized what was wrong. Angel could *see* her. The puppy only borrowed her body when she thought she could get away with it — in other words, when she thought Tasha wasn't watching.

Tasha zoomed up through the ceiling, and then poked her head back down through it just in time to see the puppy's astral form race off towards the living room. Quick as a wink, Tasha leapt down and nabbed the puppy's body.

"Tasha," her mother was saying, "stop this sulking. Tasha, get up . . ."

Tasha raced down the open door to the basement, taking the stairs at a rapid pace. She got to the storeroom door, which was closed, but she could work magic in Angel's body because Angel was magical. She waved her paw, using the keylock spell, and the door opened. She darted through.

The portal was still uncovered, swirling light and awfully small. Tasha realized for the first time that Angel was a lot bigger than she had been a few weeks ago. Would she even still fit?

Tasha took a deep breath, and then she bolted forward. There was no use hesitating.

*Squeeze squeeze squeeze — pop!*

Her stomach was sore, enough that she suspected Angel's body was a little bit bruised, but she had just barely fit. Tasha lay just to the side of the portal, panting with her tongue hanging out, and waited.

"Now, stop sulking," Sorkan Rena was saying, and there was the sound of two sets of footsteps, one of them almost being dragged. "I realize you're disappointed, but it's not like she'll be ill-treated. You can have one of the other animals for a pet later, as long as you're helpful and don't lie to me again. The tom, for instance."

*The tom!* Tasha wanted to laugh. *Even if that cat is magical, which we don't know for sure, he's a gigantic pest! No, thank you!*

The door to the storeroom closed, and her mother's voice kept lecturing from inside the room.

She snuck a peek at the edge of the portal. Had Angel noticed? Could Angel see what was near the floor? The dog seemed too agitated and worried to be noticing anything.

"Now, settle down," Sorkan Rena said. "Let me show you the first few steps inside the world. I think you'll see that's it's ideal for our needs, most of the animals being identical or similar to species on Earth . . ."

Angel suddenly went stiff. She had seen the portal. Tasha wanted to cheer.

". . . with luck, can interbreed them . . . Tasha?"

Tasha's body was wiggling its behind. Her voice barked loudly, the body went crashing backwards, and the puppy's astral form exploded out of it, racing towards the portal.

"Oh, no!" Sorkan Rena shouted. "Tasha! What did you do?"

The puppy's astral form slid through the portal, and Tasha exited her body. Reuniting her astral form with her body, Angel paused to try to lick Tasha's face, found that it didn't work, and then barked happily and stood there, wagging her tail.

A hand reached through the portal and grabbed at her.

The puppy yelped and dodged just out of reach. She barked loudly, growled angrily, and sank her teeth into the offending hand. There was a terrible scream.

Barking loudly, Angel raced off through the forest.

Desolate, Tasha watched her go with a lump in her throat. She had known that Angel would go back home eventually . . . but she'd expected to at least be able to hug her farewell. This wasn't the ending she'd expected.

The hand drew back, and Sorkan Rena was glaring furiously through the portal. "Stay right there. Don't move. I need to put a firefly through or something."

*Oh, to keep the portal open. Right, because I'm the only thing keeping it open now.* Tasha sat obediently as she heard the faint sound of her mother opening the terrarium.

But then something occurred to her.

This was an illegal portal. If it were legal, her mother wouldn't have kept it a secret. If Sorkan Rena got away with doing things illegally now, she would keep taking bigger and bigger chances, and eventually end up in jail. Tasha didn't want that.

So she jumped through the portal as her mother turned around with a firefly in hand.

The portal sealed behind her and disappeared.

"*TASHA!*" her mother screamed, her face turning red. "Can you do one single thing I ask you to?!"

Tasha slipped into her body . . .

Ugh. She felt woozy, and she had a crashing headache. Angel hadn't been very careful at all about leaving it.

"If we're going to use a portal, we have to do it legally," she said, focusing cautiously around her headache. "We can't do it illegally, Mom. That's wrong, and it's dangerous."

"Do you know what that would entail?!" her mother exclaimed. "Do you know the licensing fees, and the taxes, and the quarantines? The quarantines alone are a nightmare! You're supposed to keep an animal from another world in quarantine for six weeks to make sure they aren't carrying any diseases that aren't in our world!"

Tasha paused. That sounded . . . like a really good idea, actually. She was more convinced than ever that this was the right thing.

"It's bad enough that you keep conning those wannabes, Mom, and that's only a grey area," Tasha said carefully. "I'm willing to help, but only if you're doing things legally."

There was silence for a long moment.

"We don't have the money to do things legally," Sorkan Rena said tightly. "If we did, don't you think I would? If we had *one* provably magical animal, I could sell that to a witch, and maybe we could use that money, but you just got rid of the only one we've ever had."

Tasha looked away, uncomfortable. "Well, I'm sorry, but I had to keep my promise, and Angel was here illegally —"

She stopped.  She stared at the shelf with her jaw dropping. She couldn't believe her eyes.

". . . because you cared more about some puppy than you did about me . . ." her mother was saying furiously.

"No, Mom!" Tasha cried. "Look!  Look!"

She pointed at the locked rat cage, which was usually full of rats. Instead, there was a cat napping in there, with no rats in sight.

"That stupid tom!" Sorkan Rena exclaimed. "How in the world did he get in this room?  Much less in there?!"

Tasha exploded in giggles. "Are you *sure* we don't have a provably magical animal?  Because I think we do."

Sorkan Rena eyed the cat appraisingly.  ". . . You know what? I'll call some witches in the morning."

# Old-Fashioned

I knew my mom was old-fashioned, but I had no idea she was from the 1800s.

"Time-travel?" I said incredulously.

"That's right!" my mother chirped, gesturing at the weird, bleeping device Dad had just unearthed from our basement. "Your father found me on a mission, and we ran away together!"

"Why are you telling me this *now?*"

Dad scratched his head, looking sheepish. "Well, we sort of broke a few dozen laws, and technically you're not supposed to exist. The time cops just found out, so now they're, um, hunting us."

"Let's move to the Roman Empire next!" Mom cried.

# Proof

"Mom," I said in a strained voice, "you're *not* an elf."

She just stared at me. "Oh?" she asked. "And how can you prove that?"

"No one has to prove it! Elves don't exist!"

Mom looked puzzled. "Who told you that?"

"School!"

She sighed and shook her head.

"Can you prove that you *are?*" I challenged.

"Certainly." Mom snapped her fingers. Her African violet on the windowsill exploded out of its pot and sprawled dirty roots all across the floor.

I goggled.

"Now," Mom said smugly, "would you like to meet the dragon who eats socks out of our dryer?"

# Ogres

She hadn't asked to be assigned to the church nursery today. And the toddlers were driving her crazy. She couldn't stand it any longer.

"A taming spell," she muttered under her breath. "A taming spell . . ."

There was one that always worked on her dog. She wiggled her fingers and pointed at the two-year-olds and three-year-olds running around and throwing toys at one another.

For a moment, there was silence. Then they all turned into ogres.

She put her head in her hands. *At least their parents won't be able to tell the difference.*

# Unexpected Lastborn

I shall never forget the day Mama snubbed the witch.

It was on Dirasnaide, the last day of the year.  Mama wore her best hat and dress, reminding everybody we met that this great day was her birthday.  Never mind that it was my birthday too — never mind that I wore threadbare hand-me-downs and had no hat at all.

I hugged the back of our procession, as I always did.  Being the youngest, I was frequently forgotten or pounded on.  Mama spoiled Nadrainli, the oldest, because they'd intended her birth.  Papa bragged incessantly about all of his five sons.  But I'd been a surprise, four years after Naomi, the final daughter in a family that preferred sons.

"That's right," Mama bragged to the grocer.  "It's been thirty-five years since I chased the last witch away.  Thirty-five years!  On my seventh birthday, it was, yet I was smart enough back then to know to rid the town of witches!"

I stared at the shop window glumly.  Reuben and Lee were already inside, fighting over the last piece of penny candy in a display.  In a minute, Papa would roar in there and give both of them a wallop for their bad behavior.

Papa never walloped me.  Papa never noticed me.  I'd also never had a penny I could spend on candy.

"That's right," Mama went on, preening.  "Seventh daughter of a seventh daughter I was, a real plum for any witch to take.  But did I go?  Oh, no!  Stood my ground and spat at her, didn't I?  Proved I wouldn't take her nonsense!  Proved there was no curse upon me to become one of those things!"

Sometimes I thought there was a curse upon me.

Or rather, I *was* the curse.

*Mama and Papa should have stopped with eleven*, I thought glumly. I glanced at my sister Naomi, patting her hair in the shop window. She looked so much like Mama, so prim. *Or, better yet, ten.*

A sneering voice said from behind us, "There weren't no chance yeh was ever goin' to be onna us 'things.'"

Startled, I spun around. Mama did, too. Her face went pale with horror.

"*Witch!*" she cried, pointing.

A hideous old woman wearing a threadbare traveling cape shrugged. "As yeh say."

Mama's face turned bright red. "You've come to try to convert me to your wicked ways again! Admit it!"

The witch sneered. "Yeh can call my ways wicked if yeh want, but yeh ain't got magic, and there's no use in pretendin' yeh do. Yeh ain't a seventh daughter of a seventh daughter. Yer a seventh daughter of an *eighth*." The witch sniffed. "Now, *her* . . ."

The witch pointed a bony claw towards us. It took me a moment to realize, in horror, she was pointing at me.

"Annie?" Mama asked, her voice hoarse.

"Didn't it never occur to yeh?" The witch cackled. "Yeh got seven daughters here, same as yer ma. Can't yeh count?"

I stood ramrod still, my heart pounding. What did she mean? Did she mean me? How could that be? Nobody even noticed me!

"Ain't yeh never noticed it?" The witch cackled. "The child goes invisible! How could yeh not realize a thing like that?"

I gasped and took a step backward.

Ma's face was ashen. She said nothing.

The witch burst out in laughter. "Blind, alla yeh! Fools! Nitwits!"

"Pl-please, stop it!" I gasped. "I'm not a witch! I can't be! Mama —"

Mama's face flooded with crimson. "You will not insult me any longer. Leave, before I —"

"Insult yeh?" the witch jeered. "I ain't half-done insultin' yeh! Look! Yer seventh daughter's invisible right now!"

All heads whipped around, searching for me. I cowered in fear. Wandering eyes searched through me, not seeing me. I breathed a sigh of relief, and then I realized what this meant.

What it had always meant.

I really was a witch.

"Annie?" Ma called, sounding frightened.  "Annie?"

"Annie?" Pa roared.  "If you're a witch, I'll wallop the magic right outta ya!"

"Annie!" Lee shouted.

"Annie!" Reuben yelled.

"Annie!" Naomi hollered.

"Annie!" Nadrainli cried.

I watched them all silently, realizing for the first time that I didn't have to be a curse anymore.  I could be free.

If only I had somewhere to go.

And then I saw the witch's eyes watching me.

She knew where I was, even though no one could see me.  She was standing right there, waiting for me.  She had . . . she had *come* here for me.

Nobody had ever wanted me before.

I walked over to her and silently slipped my hand in hers.

The witch's eyes glinted.  "Good choice," she whispered.  "Happy seventh birthday.  Don't worry, I ain't nearly as wicked as I look."

"I know," I whispered back.  "I know what wicked looks like, and it's not you.  It's clean and pretty, and it wallops children."

The witch's eyes darkened at first, but then they glinted.  She became invisible too, and we walked out of town together.

I shall never forget the day Mama snubbed the witch.

It was the day I started my life.

# Zombies

Two zombies were shambling around the kitchen. Breathing heavily, I cocked my squirt gun and prepared to shoot.

*Blam!* I hit one in the head. It howled with outrage.

*Splat!* I splashed one across the back. It shrieked.

*Wham!* The first zombie reached me, moving faster than I would have believed. It grabbed the squirt gun and seized my wrist. I could smell the stench of its breath.

"Die, zombie!" I shrieked, trying to pry my hands free.

The zombie growled in its guttural, barely-intelligible language. "For just one morning, would you let your parents make their coffee in peace?"

# Identical Twits

"They're not, in fact, identical twins," I tried to explain to the teacher. Off to the side, my little brothers were fighting over a toy they both wanted. No surprise, since they had identical tastes. "I only had one brother originally. The teleporter glitched and sent back two copies of him."

"How long ago was that?" the teacher asked.

"Last week," I said.

"Too late to recycle the spare, then."

I grimaced and nodded. "My parents said there were *ethical considerations* and refused to. So I'm stuck with two little brothers now."

"It's myyyyy toyyyyyyy!" one of the boys howled.

# The Hunt

There he was!  The small male!  Gryffa dove and let out a blood-curdling shriek.

Her victim looked up and screamed.  He dodged to the right, his wings flapping desperately, but she lunged and smacked him out of the sky with her talons.

He fought back, piercing with his beak and slicing his claws at her shoulder.

She slammed him into the ground and he lay still.  She waited patiently until he groaned, and then hopped off, her tail lashing proudly.

"Okay, you win," he groaned.  "What do you want?  It's not mating season."

Gryffa purred.  "Will you be my Valentine?"

# Imaginary Fiend

"He sat on Celeste!" Susie wailed. She pointed at her brother across the room.

"Celeste?" their mother asked, befuddled. "What — your imaginary friend?"

"He sat on her, and now she's bleeding!"

"Nyah nyah," Kevin said, wriggling his bottom around on the sofa cushion as if to rub it in.

"Susie," their mother said, touching her forehead, "I'm sure Celeste is fine. Imaginary friends don't tend to get hurt if someone sits on them. In fact, I'm sure she doesn't even mind your brother —"

"What the?" Kevin yelped, jumping up and looking all around him. "Did someone invisible just kick me?"

# Karmic Balance

"My schedule's booked through November," the assassin said. "I had a target in March."

The client tried not to stare at the assassin's obviously-pregnant belly. "Is that going to get in the way?" he hedged.

"What?" The assassin looked down. "Oh, this? No. I have a baby every time I kill somebody."

The client laughed, thinking she was joking. "You must have killed a dozen people."

"Fifteen."

"So I'm sure you don't —"

She reached into her wallet and casually tossed a picture on the table.

The client paused, aghast.

"Don't you think it's good karmic balance?" the assassin said cheerfully.

# The Open Source Time-Travel App

"I believe that what you do with your time-travel is your own business," Ms. Atwin said, holding out a basket as she walked down the aisles. "But if you use it in my classroom, it's considered cheating. So, hand over your cellphones, please."

"As if I'm going to waste my daily eight minutes on tests," Chet stage-whispered to his best friend.

"I barely even use mine," Stanley shrugged, dropping his in.

"I already used mine so I wasn't late," Hannah sighed.

Ms. Atwin stopped and pulled an offending phone from the basket. "And no counterfeits from tomorrow, either!" she shouted.

# The Kraken

A merchant ship set sail
Along in the water,
And was caught by pirates.
There was a great slaughter.

They raided the rations;
They plundered the treasure.
"We had you for lunch!"
They cried with great pleasure.

They blasted their cannons.
The merchant ship drowned.
A terrible kraken
Perked up at the sound.

One desperate battle
Was only for naught.
The great kraken crunched them.
"Yum!  Dinner!" it thought.

And then the great kraken,
A sailor's worst dread,
Swam by a sea dragon.
"Mm.  Breakfast," it said.

# Author's Notes

## Valentine's Oops

## To Catch a Leprechaun

## The Goose That Laid Golden Easter Eggs

In late 2015, I received some helpful advice from the Kboards, a place where many indie authors were hanging out. An author I knew suggested writing and publishing a Christmas short story as a freebie during December. I thought that was a great idea, and I already had "The Dragon and the Santa" written, so I published it separately as a freebie. It worked out well enough that I started thinking, "What if I did something like that for every month of the year?"

I took the characters from "When the Wilkinsons Grew" and wrote these three short stories in February, March, and April. I wanted to write more and have a whole book compilation of their adventures, but then I had the idea for the Fairy Senses series in March 2016, and I realized that my time would be better spent writing a book series instead of a short story series. So I only wrote these three seasonal short stories.

## The Toddler's Lament

## I Do Not Want to Take a Nap

Sometime in 2014, when I had two one-and-a-half-year-olds who did not want to take their naps, I wrote this poem. I believe I came up with it to describe Nicodemus, though Simon was a culprit, too.

In December 2016, a woman I knew at church was making Christmas baskets for the migrant workers, and she said most of them had no books and would dearly like some. I turned the poem into a mini picture book specifically to print over 100 copies and to give one to each family.

# Little House in the Crater

My grandmother didn't like my first book, *Black Magic Academy*. She told me to write something more like *Little House on the Prairie*.

I wrote something more like *Little House on the Prairie*.

I don't think this was what she had in mind.


## MIRROR IMAGE

I wrote this for the Spring 2013 edition of *Spellbound*, "Changelings and Dopplegangers," and it was originally published there.  I thought a mirror image was a fun take on that theme.


## Knock Three Times

I wrote this poem for a special anthology of *Spellbound* that was going to have fairy tale retellings with minority main characters. (Sadly, it was never released.)  I chose to tell a version of "Cinderella" in which she has severe OCD and is her own worst enemy. Naturally, it had to be a poem, because the rhythm and structure are necessary to tell that story.


## The Reason Why My Paper is Late

Erica, my roommate in my second semester of college, had to write a one-page essay entitled "Why My Paper is Late" because she was turning in a paper late.  I said, "Ooh!  Ooh!  Can I write it for you?" She said, "Sure."

I wrote this.

I don't think it's what the professor I had mind.

# Glass Beads

I wrote this short story for a science fiction anthology called *Far Orbit* back in 2013. It didn't get accepted, and in fact just sat around collecting dust until now. It did appear in an anthology called *Rejected!* in 2015, but that was a much earlier draft that wasn't nearly as good.

## Computer Gremlins

I once had a computer that liked to randomly crash and delete things. I named it The Horror. When it had eaten several of my short stories, it was time to get rid of it.

## The Dark Lord's Genie

Don't try to pester the cranky being who grants wishes. He might try to make his own personal wish come true.

## The Day of Shoulder Angels

What if you literally had to deal with shoulder angels and demons once a year, every year? I think it would be very annoying.

## Pixie Eggs

No, this poem isn't free verse. I don't like free verse. It's a shaped poem.

I wrote a ton of poetry in high school, mainly lyrical poetry that was super preachy, much like the stuff I read in English class. Looking back at most of it, I cringe. (Though there are a rare few I still like.)

One day in 2013, I found an old notebook where I had written an odd little shaped poem called "Our Ship" that I'd never transferred to my computer. I rectified this. Then I started to think, "Hey, maybe I could write another shaped poem! That might be fun!"

"Pixie Eggs" was the first poem I had written in about seven years. I had so much fun with it that it resulted in a resurgence of poetry writing in 2013, all narrative poetry, the rest metered and rhymed.

## Miss Galaxy

As a kid, I liked to make paper dolls.  One day when I was eleven, I made something called *The Planet Paper Dolls.*  There was one beauty contestant for each planet in our solar system, all aliens except the girl from Earth, and one of them was a puddle with a bow on it. Yes, they were all paper dolls, including the puddle.  It had many different bows you could tab on.

## Way Too Familiar

I turned "The Body-Borrower" into a drabble, because it worked.

## Standardized Testing

When I was in college, I wrote a not-very-good short story about a teacher finding aliens students who were giggling during the test, and those giggles turned out to be an alien language that they were using to pass information to each other to cheat.  I shortened it.

## *The Silent Princess*

I also wrote this for the *Spellbound* anthology that sadly didn't happen. I had long thought that a version of "The Frog Prince" with a deaf princess would be cool.  It would explain why she made that crazy deal with the frog — she didn't understand what he was saying!

## Dragon Bait

I wrote this one on a whim for a micro short story competition at CONduit in 2014, a Salt Lake convention I attended every year.

## Easy Target

Even a senile wizard could be a formidable foe.  Don't irritate them.

## The Librarian is In

I badly want to write a book about this librarian sometime.

## One Midsummer's Night

The second poem I wrote in 2013.  I wrote it for the Summer 2013 edition of *Spellbound*, "Dragons," and it was originally published there. This is one of my favorite poems I've ever written.

## The Body-Borrower

A friend gave me a writing prompt: "Have you been borrowing my body again?" as a first line.  Her short story was horror.  Someone else wrote a romantic comedy with a mannequin in it.  I went with fantasy.

## Old-Fashioned

This used to be a not-very-good longer short story.  It's better now.

## Proof

The real question is: is that dragon a pet, or an unwelcome pest they can't get rid of?  It'll cost three socks to find out.

## Ogres

I've had a calling in the church nursery before.  I had two two-year-olds when I wrote this.  IT'S TRUE!

## Unexpected Lastborn

This one wound up a lot darker than usual for me.  I wrote the original draft when I was in my junior year of high school, and it's been rewritten about ten times since then.

## Zombies

I actually can't relate to this.  I don't drink coffee, or caffeine at all!

## Identical Twits

I figure those "ethical considerations" probably sound an awful lot like pro-life versus pro-choice debates.

### The Hunt

Of course gryphons give each other hearts on Valentine's Day!  Real ones.

### Imaginary Fiend

I used to take my imaginary friends very seriously.  This is pretty much exactly like something my siblings and I would have done.

### Karmic Balance

I had the idea for an assassin with a really weird code of ethics: she never takes more people out of the world than she is willing to bring into it.

It would be really weird to be one of her kids.  I don't think she tells them she is secretly an assassin.

### The Open Source Time-Travel App

I see this as a future where everyone has an app on their cellphone to allow them eight minutes of time-travel every day.  To have more, you have to pay an expensive subscription fee.

### The Kraken

There's always a bigger fish!  And in this case, that fish happens to be a dragon.

This poem was originally published in the Summer 2014 edition of *Spellbound*, "Sea Monsters," which was sadly the last edition of that magazine before it folded.

# About the Author

Emily Martha Sorensen has written over thirty fantasy books that are fun and clean. From 2012 to 2015, she published one book each year. In 2016, she had a breakthrough, and has been publishing an average of one book a month ever since.

She has four kids, a wonderful husband who is the greatest ever, and a desk treadmill that sure helps her lose weight (thanks for the pregnancies, kids!).

One of these days, she'd sure like to invent a time machine, or at least get to use one.